CAN YOU SPELL
REVOLUTION?

·CAN· YOU SPELL REVOLUTION?

matt beam

· DUTTON CHILDREN'S BOOKS ·

DUTTON CHILDREN'S BOOKS

A division of Penguin Young Readers Group

PUBLISHED BY THE PENGUIN GROUP

Penguin Group (USA) Inc., 375 Hudson Street, New York, New York 10014, U.S.A. • Penguin Group (Canada), 90 Eglinton Avenue East, Suite 700, Toronto, Ontario M4P 2Y3, Canada (a division of Pearson Penguin Canada Inc.) • Penguin Books Ltd, 80 Strand, London WC2R 0RL, England • Penguin Ireland, 25 St Stephen's Green, Dublin 2, Ireland (a division of Penguin Books Ltd) • Penguin Group (Australia), 250 Camberwell Road, Camberwell, Victoria 3124, Australia (a division of Pearson Australia Group Pty Ltd) • Penguin Books India Pvt Ltd, 11 Community Centre, Panchsheel Park, New Delhi - 110 017, India • Penguin Group (NZ), 67 Apollo Drive, Rosedale, North Shore 0632, New Zealand (a division of Pearson New Zealand Ltd.) • Penguin Books (South Africa) (Pty) Ltd, 24 Sturdee Avenue, Rosebank, Johannesburg 2196, South Africa • Penguin Books Ltd, Registered Offices: 80 Strand, London WC2R 0RL, England

This book is a work of fiction. Names, characters, places, and incidents are either the product of the author's imagination or are used fictitiously, and any resemblance to actual persons, living or dead, business establishments, events, or locales is entirely coincidental.

CIP Data is available.

Published in the United States by Dutton Children's Books, a division of Penguin Young Readers Group
345 Hudson Street, New York, New York 10014
www.penguin.com/youngreaders

Designed by Jason Henry

Printed in USA • First Edition
ISBN: 978-0-525-47998-7

1 3 5 7 9 10 2 6 4 2

TO YOUNG REBELS
WOLFGANG, ROCKY AND KINNIE
—M.B.

• ACKNOWLEDGMENTS •

I want to thank my early readers and tireless supporters: Michelle, Joe, Al, Matty, Katie, Joanne, and RT. Thanks also to Marie Campbell, David and Lynn Bennett, and Sarah Shumway. Special thanks to Sara Beam for historical guidance and sisterly love. Finally, thanks to Lorraine for accepting Clouds et al. into her life many moons ago.

CAN YOU SPELL
REVOLUTION?

Prologue

Rules. They were what he hated most. He hated them more than bubble gum on his shoe. He hated them more than Mrs. Topper's suspicious gaze. He might have even hated them more than Principal Dorfman's nasty accusations. Rules, Clouds said, were the root of all evil. And believe me, when Clouds McFadden said something, he meant it.

· PART 1 ·
Mysterious Clouds

I s there a word that means "bored out of your brains and totally powerless"?

I doubt it, but that's exactly how I felt sitting in the first school assembly of second term this year. Not only was I stuck in the worst, most torturous part of the school week, I had somehow gotten myself trapped between Mrs. Topper, my strict eighth grade teacher, and her favorite student, Sally Walder, at the back of the auditorium. It was the first week of the second term, so Principal Dorfman—also known as the Penguin because he waddled through the hallways—was outlining his plans for the coming year at Laverton Middle School.

". . . And so for the good of *your* education," he said into the microphone on the podium, "and for the good of the education of the students to your left and for the good of the education of the students to your right and for the good of the education of the students in front of you, I'm going to review a few school rules with you."

On one side of the auditorium, I could see Doug, my old best friend, goofing around with a couple of his football friends, right under the nose of Mr. Evans, their easygoing teacher. Doug and I are in different classes this year because Mom called the school in the summer, insisting that we be separated. Mr. Singh, our teacher from seventh grade, had convinced Mom that D-student Doug was the cause of my low grades last year. It was as good a guess as any, I suppose.

And then, in September, things got even worse for Doug and me. I didn't want to try out for the football team, but I told him that Mom was making me come home to study every afternoon. After he made the team, Doug started acting way too cool and basically ignored me when any of his football friends were around. Not that I cared much.

The Penguin raised his voice slightly, which caught my attention.

". . . And what that means, students, is that the School Notice Collector from each class, and *only* the School Notice Collector from each class, may come down to the office to retrieve the school notices. His or her best friend *may not* replace the School Notice Collector without permission from the teacher, and, no, his or her best friend *may not* accompany the School Notice Collector to the office. Only, and I repeat, *only* the School Notice Collector has permission to leave class. . . ."

My eye caught some movement on the other side of the auditorium. It was Harriet Frost and Alita Merle, giggling and pointing at some poor seventh grader who was sporting an unfortunate bowl cut. Harriet and Alita had become the obvious leaders of the long-standing and exclusive Laverton Middle School club called the Magnas. The Magnas were basically the most popular eighth grade girls. Most of the students knew that ten seventh grade girls were chosen to be Magnas at the end of the year by the current members, but it wasn't like there was PA announcement about it. You could spot the new group by the gold pins they wore, which were in the shape of an M.

This year it was clear that Harriet and Alita were trying to make their Magna membership a big deal. In October, the two girls held a loud and public Magna meeting at the center of the basketball court, which made it evident to the other eight members that *they* were in charge. Everyone heard about it, and so the whole school was introduced to the new and not-so-improved Magnas. If there was something you owned that the Magnas wanted—or simply didn't want you to have—you were definitely going to find out about it—quickly. Seventh-grader Claire Soles was their first serious victim when she risked walking home with handsome Zach "the Quarterback" two days in a row. The Magnas weren't about to declare their collective and unconditional love for cool guys like Zach, but they also weren't going to let anyone else get near him. A rumor about Claire's bad breath soon made it onto the walls of the girl's bathroom, and before you knew it, even fifth graders were calling Claire "Stinky-Breath Soles." Zach wasn't the kind of guy to risk his popularity for a cute but insignificant seventh grader, which I'm sure the Magnas had counted on.

I saw Claire sitting a couple of rows in front of me in assembly, her shoulders slumped. She still hadn't recovered from crossing the Magnas' path.

I sighed and looked out the auditorium windows. The January sky was so dull and gray that you could just barely see tiny flakes, which looked more like rain than snow.

I was just beginning to count my lucky stars that I was inside and warm instead of outside and cold, when Mrs. Topper's voice penetrated my thoughts.

"Chris," she hissed, pointing to the front. "Sit up and pay attention."

I sighed again, slowly straightened up, and looked to the front. Principal Dorfman was gone, and Susan Miranda was reading the student council minutes. Susan's voice was nice to listen to. She was a Magna, but I couldn't remember her being in the middle of any of this year's trouble. Unlike Harriet and Alita, Susan was always on the honor roll, and was involved in all kinds of activities like the student council, the Stop Poverty Drive, and the girls' soccer team, yet somehow managed not to rub this success in anyone's face, and was cool enough to hang with the Magnas. She was way, way out of my league.

I leaned back and decided that if I had to endure more assembly, I might as well try to enjoy it. I blocked out the details of the student council minutes and listened to Susan's peaceful voice. It was a calm before the storm, before the mysterious Clouds moved suddenly into my life.

2

When I stepped into class I froze in my tracks. There was a smiling kid with red hair sitting in Mrs. Topper's seat *with his feet on her desk*! I hustled to my seat, and watched carefully as other students came in as I had, stopped in their shoes, and then scurried to their seats. When Landry Colburn strode into the room, his eyes bulged and he gestured to the stranger like he was slitting his throat. Normally Mrs. Topper would have had her eye on Landry, but we knew she was still dealing with Terrence Fripp, who had been making trouble in the hall. When Mrs. Topper's final scolds echoed outside the door, Landry rushed to his seat and the class went silent.

Just before she appeared the redhead smiled, dropped his feet, and sat up. We all watched as Mrs. Topper stopped in the doorway, her eyes narrowed, and her neck flushed to her earlobes.

The boy continued to wear his mysterious smile.

Mrs. Topper strode up and stood in front of him with her hands on her hips. "May I help you?" She glared at him.

"I'm Clouds," he said. "Clouds McFadden."

"Oh, yes . . . Clouds," Mrs. Topper murmured. "I don't suppose you mind if I sit, Mr. McFadden?"

"By all means," Clouds said, with a wink and smile at the class. This triggered a subdued class giggle, accompanied by Landry's guffawing laugh.

"Excuse me," Mrs. Topper said to the class, and then scowled at Landry. "Just what is so funny?"

"Um, well," Landry said, "he sort of looked at us and winked and his eyebrows kind of went like this and I don't know, it's funny how that happens sometimes, you don't even know why you are laughing and—"

"Landry," she interrupted.

"What?" he asked.

"It was a *rhetorical* question."

"What's a rhetorical question?"

"It means, Landry," Boris spoke up, from the back of the room, pushing his oversized glasses up the bridge of his oversized nose, "that Mrs. Topper didn't really want an answer."

"Boris Bergman," Mrs. Topper snapped. "You know the rules—hand up if you want to speak."

"I was only trying to help."

"Well, you help when you follow the rules."

Boris's hand shot up.

"Yes, Boris."

"Why isn't my chess club advertisement on the Class Events Board anymore?"

"Your what? Oh . . . I needed space for the February field trip, Boris. Now—"

"But I just put it there yesterday!"

"Boris! Not now," she snapped, turning back to the new student. "In the future, Mr. McFadden—"

"Oh, feel free to call me Clouds," he interjected coolly, facing the class again with that sly smile.

Mrs. Topper's face burned. "In the future, Mr. McFadden," she repeated, "you will kindly sit in the seat that is assigned to you." She pointed to the empty seat in the back corner of the room.

"Sure," he replied.

And then the new kid did something none of us had ever seen a kid do with any teacher at Laverton Middle School: he put out his hand to shake.

Mrs. Topper glanced down at his outstretched hand dismissively.

"By the way," he said, smiling at her and then at the rest of the class, "it's a real pleasure to be in your class."

"Thank you." Mrs. Topper's lips were pursed, her face now beet red. "Now then class," she said, clearing her throat. "By now you know that we have a new student joining us. Meet Clouds McFadden."

There was silence in the class as he turned toward us, and I took a good look at him. Clouds had a wild tuft of thick red hair, and he was just a little short of average height. He had mysterious and intense gray eyes, like ones you might see on the face of an arctic wolf on an educational TV program. Scattered around these two icy moons was a constellation of reddish-brown freckles. His mouth was wide with thick lips, which spread out in a great big smile.

What was weirdiest about him was he didn't look at his shoes timidly like other new students did. He peered around the room as if he were an army sergeant looking for recruits. After I recovered from the intensity of his eyes passing mine, I glanced around the class for other people's reactions. I saw Magnas Sherry Linton, Zigi Cates, Emma Rothman, and Maria Borelli eyeing each other like they just couldn't figure this guy out—and that they needed to, quickly. I saw the black-haired and mean-spirited Sherry take out a piece of paper and start scribbling notes. Landry, the hyperactive bane of Mrs. Topper's existence, sat at the front, his long legs splayed, his head back, his mouth open in awe. Clouds smiled that smile toward the back of the corner of the classroom, where Boris was not deep into a science fiction novel as per usual but was staring back blankly, as if he couldn't figure something out for once.

Clouds maintained his gaze and cleared his throat.

"Good day, fellow proletariats," he said, still smiling and surveying the room. His voice was deep for his age. "I'm really looking forward to the rest of the year here at Laverton Middle School."

There was an awkward silence, and then a few more giggles.

Mrs. Topper's brow furrowed. "All right, Clouds," she said. "Just take your seat and we'll get on with the day."

Clouds nodded and strode to the back of the class. There was a knock at the door, and the Penguin stepped into the room.

"Mr. Dorfman," Mrs. Topper said warmly. "What can I do for you?"

"Is Clouds McFadden here?"

"Right here, Principal Dorfman," Clouds said, still standing. "Is there a problem?" he asked with a grin.

Principal Dorfman turned and stared. There was silence. I saw Landry mouth *uh-oh*, because we all knew what was coming.

"Raise your hand if you want to speak, young man!" the Penguin snapped. "I know Mrs. Topper expects hands-up in her classroom, and I expect the same."

"Yes, Mr. Dorfman," Clouds said cheerfully. "No problem."

"Now, Mr. McFadden, did you sign in at the office like you were asked to?"

"Um, no, because no one was there when—"

"If no one is in the office, people," the Penguin interrupted, looking around the room, "what does a student do?"

Sally Walder's arm shot up.

"Yes, Sally."

"You wait in the Waiting Area, which is right beside the office. There are three seats, and if there are more than three people waiting, you must stand beside the third seat until one is available."

The Penguin smiled and nodded. "Very good, Sally."

"I know, I *did* wait," Clouds argued, "but the place was deserted, and then I figured I knew which room to go to and—"

"Mr. McFadden! Your hand!"

I saw Magnas Sherry, Zigi, Marie, and Emma snicker.

The Penguin took a deep breath, and shook his head. "At Laverton Middle School, Mr. McFadden," he continued, "instead of having students 'figure,' we have them follow *rules*. And if the rules are followed, then everything runs smoothly, and if everything runs smoothly, then we don't have to waste everyone's *time* and *education*."

Clouds just stared at the Penguin.

"Do I make myself clear?"

"Yes."

"Yes, what?"

"Yes, you make yourself clear."

The Penguin pursed his lips. "You mean, 'Yes, sir.' At Laverton Middle School, young man, students may use Mr., Mrs., Miss, or Ms. plus a surname, or 'sir' for men, 'ma'am' for women. Understood?"

"Yes," Clouds said, pausing for a second. "Sir."

The Penguin's eyes bulged. "I know for a fact, Mr. Mc-Fadden, that you received the school handbook weeks ago." His eyes scanned the room. "I would advise you and your peers to know the school rules, or you will find yourself in a lot of trouble this term." He turned to Mrs. Topper. "Forgive the interruption. Please continue."

The Penguin waddled to the door and all of us, including Mrs. Topper, listened as he squeaked down the hallway.

At break I had to go to the library to return a book, so I was late getting outside. When I got to the top of the school steps, I looked around: it had stopped snowing, and there was serious excitement in the school grounds. Word of the new kid in Mrs. Topper's class was spreading. Groups of eighth graders were blotched around in conspiratorial clumps. On the snow-covered basketball court, Sherry appeared to be giving an animated account of Clouds's remarkable arrival to the concerned Harriet and Alita. A large group of snow fort makers, who had been busy since a major snowstorm a week earlier, were packing blocks in the gully, but a few scouts kept an eye on both the new boy and the commotion he'd started. Even Doug and the football guys huddled and pointed over at Clouds before they started a game on the snowy field.

I watched as Clouds walked around the school grounds, seemingly unfazed by the buzz he'd created. For the most part, Clouds was observing people from a distance, but he stopped several times to look down at the ground and kick at the snow as if he were thinking something through.

Then suddenly, to my complete amazement, the new kid swiveled around and looked in *my* direction.

My heart stopped.

I turned to see if there was anyone behind me. No one. I turned back.

Was Clouds looking at *me*? I couldn't know for sure. He was wearing that same grin and didn't move a muscle. He was definitely looking in my direction. I felt seriously scrutinized, but I couldn't understand why—what interest could he have in me?

As I descended the steps, I watched as Clouds turned and strode confidently toward the Magnas. This kid had absolutely no idea of the pit of snakes he was about to drop into. When he got to the Magnas, Clouds literally broke through the crowd, interrupting the girls with raised hands and words I couldn't hear.

I needed to get within earshot. I pretended I was heading to the snow forts, but had my ears on high alert.

". . . and I saw the beautiful pins you four were wearing in Mrs. Topper's class, and I figured you must all be in some sort of special club."

"We're Magnas," Alita declared, tucking her short blond hair behind her ears. "Who wants to know?"

I stopped and turned when the girls' backs were to me, and I thought I saw Clouds glance and smile my way for a split second before he continued.

"I'm Clouds, Clouds McFadden," he said, crossing his arms, his eyes now switching back and forth between Harriet and Alita, "and I just wanted you to know that if you ever need assistance I'm—"

"And, like, we need your help?" Alita sneered. A couple of Magnas looked at each other and giggled, as Alita nudged Harriet for support.

Clouds appeared unfazed as Harriet ignored Alita, crossed *her* arms, and angled her head at the new student. There was an awkward silence. The rest of the girls were clearly unsettled by this strange new student, and the fact that their leader wasn't verbally tearing him to shreds.

"Well, anyway, Harriet, ladies, it was a real pleasure to meet all of you," he said, with a smile.

"It was, um, nice to meet you, too," Harriet murmured.

He smiled at her once more, nodded at the other girls respectfully, and strode past Harriet and Alita . . . toward me.

As the Magnas' eyes turned my way, I felt my stomach tighten. What was Clouds planning now, and what could it possibly have to do with me? With every step he took, I could feel my palms going clammy. My face felt hot. I looked up to face Clouds only to see him give me a sly nod as he continued past.

Without even looking back toward the Magnas, I put my head down and hurried away to the snow forts to gather myself. I was sure this new kid was up to something. I could feel it.

The next few days at school were full of the same odd behavior from Clouds McFadden. One morning, right after Mrs. Topper had handed out one of her notorious time-killing worksheets, Clouds and Boris were told to stop talking once. And then again. And then a third and final time.

"Boys!" Mrs. Topper said, putting down her pen and standing up. "Why don't you share what's *so important* with the rest of the class?"

Boris looked down at his worksheet and shrugged. Clouds smiled and cleared his throat. "Well, Mrs. Topper," he began, "the brilliant and under-utilized Boris Berg-man was telling me how much he absolutely loved doing these . . . these wonderful, wonderful—"

Clouds stopped speaking because Boris had whipped around in his seat, and his face was burning red. Clouds shrugged at the bespectacled brainiac, and whispered something under his breath, which caused Boris to turn even redder. He slowly turned back to Mrs. Topper.

"Um, yes, well, Mrs. Topper," Boris stammered. "I don't mean to be rude, and I know I can be, but I was just say-ing to, um, *him*, that perhaps we might, um, be doing something sort of, more challenging than another one of these, um, worksheets."

"Bah!" Landry laughed, then covered his mouth and ducked as if this would help him escape punishment. I noticed Sherry and Emma, who sat one in front of the other in the middle of the classroom, giggling carefully into their hands.

Mrs. Topper bored down on Landry. "That's one detention, Mr. Colburn."

"Oh, man!" Landry said, his head dropping. "It's not like I meant to. I just can't help it sometimes."

"That's not good enough, Landry, and you know it," she said.

Landry slouched in his seat angrily, and Mrs. Topper looked to the back of the room.

"I'm sorry, Boris," Mrs. Topper said, "I must have missed something. Did you get a degree in teaching while the rest of us weren't looking?"

"Um, no, but," Boris said, "I just . . . it's just . . . it's just that we always—"

"That's more than enough, Mr. Bergman, unless you'd like to turn the worksheet into a surprise test, which will be added to your report cards, which I'm in the process of finalizing."

I saw Terrence and several other students stiffen and shake their heads at Boris. Clouds was scribbling in his notebook.

"No, no," Boris said, waving his hands in front of him. "This is just fine . . . perfect even. I'm sorry, Mrs. Topper. Really. I don't know where my head is today."

Mrs. Topper stared at Boris for a moment, then said, "Fine. Get to work everyone. I expect complete silence until the bell."

The bell rang an hour later, and as I was walking down the corridor I saw Clouds with his arm around Landry. The redhead was whispering in Landry's ear and for once my hyperactive classmate was listening. Clouds peeled off to the washroom, and Landry tore off down the corridor. When I exited the school doors, I thought I'd do the usual: kill time, stay out of trouble, and partake in my new favorite pastime, covert Clouds-watching.

It didn't take long before there was something to watch. Terrence had started trouble. He was holding a soccer ball up in the air near the jungle gym, and a crowd of younger students was trying to get it back from him. I saw Susan Miranda heading in Terrence's direction as the rest of the Magnas, including Harriet and Alita, trailed behind her. I jumped down the stairs and jogged toward the action. It took me a moment to realize there was someone jogging right beside me: it was Clouds.

"It's Chris, right?" he said, smiling.

"Um, yeah," I replied, smiling back.

"Well, Chris, my friend," he said, speeding ahead, "get ready to watch a short episode of 'The Young and the Powerless.'"

He broke through the crowd like before and I pushed my way through to the front for a good view.

Susan was already in mid-argument with Terrence when Clouds and I arrived. I expected him to bust into the conversation as he had done with the Magnas, but he just stood there with his arms crossed and watched.

". . . And like I said, those balls are for the younger grades," Susan stated, clearly frustrated. "I'm on the student council, Terrence, and I'm a part of making these kinds of decisions."

"So?" Terrence said, shrugging.

"Give it back, turd brain," Alita said, stepping forward and trying to knock it out of his hands. "Or else."

"Or else what?" Terrence demanded, holding the ball over his head. The Magnas' power was in popularity, mind games, and social strategy, all of which went right over Terrence's head.

Alita looked back at Harriet for backup but she simply yawned and looked at her nails. "Don't we have bigger fish to fry, Magnas?"

"Um, yeah, Magnas," Alita said, looking desperately for Harriet's approval.

I saw Susan's shoulders sink, and then Clouds stepped forward. "Terr, I get it. I *totally* get what you are saying."

"Um . . . what am I saying?" Terrence asked, lowering the ball. Harriet and Alita stopped to listen.

"The rules!" Clouds exclaimed, his arms thrown in the air. "I really, really can't stand them. There's a stupid rule for everything."

"You got that right, brotha," Terrence said, smiling. "Rules suck."

"But the thing is," Clouds said, stepping closer to Terrence. "It just looks bad."

"What looks bad?" Terrence asked, furrowing his brow.

"The whole playing-with-little-kids thing," Clouds said, so that everyone could hear.

"What do mean 'playing with little kids'?" Terrence demanded angrily, his hand with the ball in it dropping to his side.

"Hey look, Terr," Clouds said, pointing his thumb at his own chest, "*I* know you aren't playing with little kids, but from a distance, I'm sorry to say, it really does look that way."

Terrence looked around at the fifth graders surrounding him.

"And Harriet's right," he said, winking at the Magnas' leader, who responded with a reserved smile. "If you are going for real power, why bother with little minnows when there are bigger fish to fry?"

"What do you mean?" Terrence asked.

"Look around you," Clouds replied, putting an arm around Terrence and trailing his other arm in an arc over the schoolyard as if it was an ocean of possibility.

"*Riiight,*" Terrence said. "Bigger fish." He nodded in understanding, his wide eyes gazing at the playground as if seeing the potential.

"Like," Clouds said, pointing, "at least the sixth graders playing over there. They look like they're more your speed."

A brave fifth grader suddenly snatched the ball from

under Terrence's arm and ran a safe distance away. Terrence stepped to chase her, but Clouds grabbed him by the arm.

"Remember, Terr," he said softly. "You don't want to be known as a minnow chaser, do you? Carrying around a net on your shoulder and a little jar in your hand?"

Harriet and Zigi giggled.

"Right," Terrence said, nodding and stepping toward the forts. "The sixth graders."

"At *least*," Clouds called out as Terrence ran off.

"Can we go now, Magnas?" Alita demanded, looking at Harriet for permission. "I think I'm actually dying of boredom."

"Yeah, seriously," Harriet allowed, but she couldn't take her eyes off Clouds. I noticed Susan also staring at Clouds, who was now looking at me.

He gave me a wink and smile, and as if he had it all timed, the bell rang to call us back to class. Clouds didn't head toward school though. He turned and strode toward Terrence, who had found his much bigger fish ten feet away: Landry was in an armlock on the ground and Terrence was giving him a first-class face wash.

Back inside, I went to my seat and got out my books. Mrs. Topper wasn't in the room yet, and the rest of my classmates were buzzing about something. Sherry and Emma were pointing at the Class Events Board and whispering. Tacked to the bottom of the board was a sign written in marker.

It said, WHOSE BOARD IS THIS ANYWAY?

Clouds and Landry entered the room. Moments later, Mrs. Topper strode in.

"Sorry for the delay, students," she said, dropping a box onto her desk. She busied herself for a moment and then looked up.

"My, my, everyone is unusually quiet."

We all kept our eyes forward, and no one spoke up.

"Well, good," she said. "Then you are ready to work. Get your social studies books out, and we'll begin."

Mrs. Topper asked Maria to read aloud from the text. I opened my book but kept my eyes on our teacher as she did her usual paces around the classroom while Maria read. It didn't take long for her to notice the Class Events Board. I watched as her neck began to flush, and her eyes turned to Clouds at the back corner of the room. I didn't dare look back myself. She walked to the board and carefully removed the two tacks that were holding the sign up. She folded it meticulously, walked to her desk, and slid it into her binder.

And that was the end of that.

3

I found a mysterious envelope on the floor of my locker at the end of the day. "Chris Stren" was typed on the front with what looked like worn-out typewriter keys. Inside was a letter, also typed, but it looked photocopied. It said:

Dear Proletariet,

Are you bored? Tired of tyrants controling everything? Sick of school subjects and stricked teachers? Wondering when it will be your turn to have the power at Laverton Middle School?

You are not alone.

Meet at the school baseball diamond at 4 p.m. on Thursday and don't let anyone know you are coming.

Today was Thursday. I looked around—Clouds was nowhere to be seen. Harriet and Alita were talking to Doug, who pretended not to see me, and Zach, his new best friend. I saw Boris stuffing books in his bag, but he looked just as uninterested in humanity as ever. Everyone else was just doing the same old thing—talking, loading backpacks, slamming overstuffed lockers closed, and *not* paying attention to me. I looked back at the note. Whatever this was, it was stupid. Probably some practical joke or something. I crumpled up the letter and stuffed it into my bag. I hurried down the hallway and started making my way home.

I crossed the snow covered playing field, looking at the empty ball diamond as I left. The school buses were revving up to leave. I went through the school gates and walked along Sunnydale Street, straight into town to where we live above Dad's carpentry shop, more of a drop-in workshop than a store. I strolled by our next-door neighbor, Bella's Needles & Yarn, and then looked into Dad's unlit workshop. No one was there, so I trudged up the alley to our back stairs.

I stopped before I climbed the first step.

What was I going to do when I got home? Watch boring TV? Play the same old computer games alone in my attic room? If Dad was there, I could pretend to study upstairs in my room. If Mom was there, it would be tedious homework downstairs on the dining room table. But Mom had been working the late shift at the hospital, so it would probably be Dad. It didn't matter. Even if I was free to do whatever I wanted, I had no idea what that was.

I took off my gloves and opened the flap of my bag. I felt around for the ball of paper, pulled it out, and slowly uncrumpled it.

One line stood out: Are you bored?

That was an understatement.

I stuffed the note into my bag, put my gloves back on, and headed back toward school.

I walked through the school gates just before dusk. I spotted four figures at the backstop by home plate and walked nervously toward them. As I approached, I felt my nervous pulse ringing in my ears. I was sure the figure in the black trench coat was Clouds.

"It's Chris," I heard a spindly shadow say. It was Landry. "Maybe he'll actually say something this year."

"Hi, Landry," I said.

"I . . . can't . . . believe . . . it," Landry said, grabbing his chest and falling back onto the snow. "The guy actually spoke."

The other three faces became clear: it was Clouds, Boris, and to my total shock, Susan Miranda from the Magnas. Seeing Susan made me feel even more nervous.

"Yes, Landry," Clouds said, his breath billowing out like smoke. "Chris is quiet, but perceptive and smart. I can tell."

I shrugged in Clouds's direction, but didn't look into his eyes.

"Okay, this is great," Clouds announced to all of us. "Now that we're all here, I would first like to congratulate you on the risky decision that all of you have just made."

"Clouds," Susan said impatiently, holding up her note. "I haven't made any decision, and if this is some sort of trick or something, I'd rather not be a part of it."

"It's no trick, Susan," he answered confidently. "I promise. I'm just trying to bring together some of the most daring, open-minded, and creative people in our school."

Daring? Creative? I thought, kicking the snow.

"Open-minded?" Boris said out loud. "I think you might have the wrong guy."

"Yeah," Landry said, now sitting on the snowy ground, his arms wrapped around his bent legs. "Try closed . . . craniumed."

But Boris wasn't paying attention. "I knew your calling us 'proletariats' the first day had to mean *something*," he said, wagging a finger at Clouds. "And then there was the note I got four days ago."

"Four days ago?" Landry exclaimed. "I got it two days ago, and I've been scratching my head ever since."

"I got mine at lunch," Susan said.

"Mine was in my locker this afternoon," I added.

Boris eyes widened. "I think I get it. Clouds didn't want there to be a commotion so he spread the notes out over a couple of days. Hmm . . . good thinking, but why didn't you want commotion?"

"I'll explain," Clouds said, grinning, "if you like."

"Please," Susan said, joining Landry on the ground, using her bag as a seat. The rest of us did the same.

Clouds cleared his throat. "I'll start at the beginning," he said. "I just moved here with my mom. We're *always* moving. So, anyway, I've been to a lot of different schools."

"All right, so you've s-s-s-seen some schools!" Landry challenged, shivering impatiently. "Wh-wh-what does that have to do with us?"

"Good point, Landry," he said, smiling. "I like questions, they're much, much better than rules. Rules are the root of all evil." He paused. "Anyway, at every single school I've been to, the students get pushed around."

"That sounds familiar," Landry said. "Yep, I believe that's exactly what Terrence was doing to me at lunch time."

"No, Landry, it's not bullies like Terrence I'm talking about," Clouds said, rubbing his black gloves together. "When it comes to students, it's actually groups like the Magnas that can really make things difficult."

Susan shrugged and looked away. I still didn't know why Clouds had picked me, and I still couldn't believe I was sitting beside Susan Miranda.

"But the *real* problem," Clouds continued, "is the adults. *They* make the rules and *we* have to follow them." He looked at us all one by one. "Take, for example, the Class Events Board in Mrs. Topper's room. Who's that board for?"

"The students, man!" Landry said with exasperation.

"Exactly!" Clouds stated.

"It was you who put up the sign!" Boris exclaimed. "I knew it was you, Clouds, but you were so poker faced."

"What sign?" Susan said.

"Just wait a second, Suz," Clouds said, raising a finger. "Mrs. Topper's Class Events Board is for the students, but the students don't really get to use it the way they want to, do they, Boris?"

"No," Boris said, shaking his head. "My chess club announcement didn't even stay up for twenty-four hours."

"Sounds familiar," Susan said, nodding. "I was in Mrs. Topper's class last year when she taught seventh grade, and I can't remember anyone using it except for her."

"I get it!" Boris exclaimed. "As . . . um . . . an act of *dissent* against Mrs. Topper's unfair policy, you put that sign up." He smiled. "I think I'm beginning to figure you out, Clouds McFadden."

"I don't know about that," Clouds said, grinning.

"I still have no idea what anyone is talking about," Landry complained.

"Landry, relax," I said. "All Boris means is that Clouds put up the notice to show the rest of us that we should use the Class Events Board ourselves instead of always leaving it to Mrs. Topper. He was trying to make a point or, as Boris calls it, an act of dissent."

"Exactly, Chris," he said, nodding. "Perfect."

His praise made me blush.

"And I *love* the name Acts of Dissent!" Clouds said suddenly to the darkening sky. "That's exactly why we're here.

I want to change things around this place, with Acts of Dissent."

"Clouds, there are other ways of changing things at school," Susan said, beginning to sound uninterested. "You should take it up with the student council. I'm the treasurer this year."

"Nope," Clouds said. "Not going to go that way. The school council is like a government, and it takes too long for anything to happen in government." He hit his fist in his palm. "We want swift action."

"Swift action!" Landry perked up. "Now yer talkin' my language. Will we be like spies?"

"Yes, in a way, we are going to have to be just as daring and sly," Clouds answered in earnest.

"Espionage," Boris said, smiling. "Very intriguing."

"Sounds like trouble," said Susan. She turned to me. "What do you think, Chris?"

All the blood seemed to rush to my head. She knew my name? *The* Susan Miranda—smart, beautiful, popular—knew *my* name! I felt a little dizzy.

"Hello? Chris? Earth to Chris! Come in Chris!" Landry was waving his hand in front of my face.

"Oh, sorry—right," I mumbled. "Well . . . I'm still here, aren't I?"

"Great," Clouds said. "Okay, so a couple of years ago, my dad started teaching me all this revolutionary stuff. He told me about this guy from a long time ago, Karl Marx, who thought he could change the world with his ideas. He believed that everybody should be equal, that everybody was just as important as everybody else. He also thought he had figured out a way of making this happen."

"Cool," I said.

"Yeah, but it's not just Karl Marx. My dad taught me about different leaders from all around the world who had their own ideas about how to make things different; how to say to the ruling tyrants who made life miserable: WE'RE NOT GOING TO TAKE IT!"

"Ohh-kay," Landry chimed in. "But what does this have to do with us?"

"Think about it. Tyrants are people who take all the power for themselves and don't share it with anybody. Sound like anyone you know, Landry?"

Landry's eyes lit up. "It's *Mr.* Colburn. Actually, *Sir* to you, young man," he said, making his voice deep. "Or if you prefer you may call me *Your Highness*."

He thumbed his nose in the air and waddled back and forth until we were all laughing hysterically.

"Exactly!" Clouds said, smiling. "And what about teachers? Have you ever met one that wasn't at least a little bit of a tyrant?"

"Mrs. Topper is pretty power hungry," Boris agreed. "She makes life miserable for every single one of her students every year. Those stupid worksheets, no talking out of turn, no putting anything on the Class Events Board."

This got me thinking.

"Whose board is it, anyway?" Boris continued, with

mounting frustration. "It should be ours, too, right? We should have the right to use it, shouldn't we?"

Until now, Clouds had been sitting back quietly, arms folded, and grinning. He sprang to his feet.

"See?! This is exactly what Karl Marx and those other leaders have to do with us! It's time for a change, comrades, and it's up to us to make it happen."

We looked around at each other, everyone nodding in enthusiastic agreement. I could feel an energy that seemed to charge the air around us, feeding our excitement.

"Imagine what's possible," he continued. "If you could change one thing at school, what would it be?"

"Sherry's perfume?" Landry suggested. "It's soooooo smelly."

"I think he means important stuff, Landry," Susan chided with a smile.

"Right," Clouds said, standing up. "I want all of you to think about three things tonight. One: do the students in our class and in our school have enough power around here? Two: if you could change one thing at school, what would it be? And three: are you willing to take the chance to make these 'Acts of Dissent' with me?" He paused, looking around at all of us. "I'll be here the same time tomorrow. When you come, keep a low profile, and don't talk to each other at school. If anyone sees Landry and Boris gabbing like friends, they'll definitely know something's up."

"Don't worry about it," Boris said dryly.

"Yeah," Landry agreed. "I'd rather get another face wash from Terrence."

Clouds smiled, nodded and then walked away across the field.

The group sat silently for a moment.

"So," I said, looking at Boris. "What do you think?"

"Well," he said in an unusually quiet voice. "He definitely has a point about some of the teachers, but I don't know what he's going to do about it."

"Yeah, and I don't want to get in any trouble," Susan piped in, "and I definitely don't know what the Magnas are going to think about all this."

"Forget about the Magnas," Landry said. "Harriet and Alita are the *worst*. And I don't know anything about this acts of distaste business, but let's face it, this is probably going to be the most exciting thing that happens to us all year."

"What about you, Chris?" Susan asked.

"Um . . . I don't know," I said, awkwardly, and blushed as she looked at me. "It does sound a bit crazy, but it also sounds kind of cool, which is more than I can say about, well, the rest of my life."

"Yer darned right, Christopher Stren," Landry yelled, falling back again and looking up to the sky. "One thing's for certain, boys and girls, I'm soooo in!"

4

"Hey there, Chris," Dad said as I stepped into our apartment. He was wearing an apron and stirring some boiling pasta. "Dinner'll be ready in a couple of minutes. Your mom's at the hospital. Would you mind setting the table?"

"Sure," I said. I grabbed the cutlery and plates, and put them on the table, returning for butter and salt and pepper.

"You gonna stay a while?" Dad asked.

"What do you mean?"

"Your coat," he said, smiling. "Are you going take it off?"

"Oh yeah," I said, shaking my head. I couldn't get Clouds McFadden and the meeting out of my mind.

When we finally sat down, I ate quickly and quietly.

"What's up, Crick?" Dad asked. He called me "Crick" because that was the way I pronounced "Chris" when I was younger. I was fine with the nickname so long as he didn't dare call me that in public.

"Nothing," I said.

"How was school today?"

"It was . . . school."

Dad shrugged and dug into his food.

"Hey, Dad?

"Yep," he said, looking up.

"Do you know what a tyrant is?"

"A tyrant, a tyrant," he said, scratching his chin. "It's funny you should ask that because my father, your grand-father, Michael David Stren, always used to say—"

"Dad, no long stories, please," I entreated. "I just want to know what a tyrant is."

"Okay, well let's see," he said, thinking for a moment. "As far as I know, a tyrant is a person, usually a leader, who uses his—or her—power too forcefully, and doesn't allow others to participate. But you know, come to think of it, when—"

"Dad," I broke in. "So . . . could, like, a teacher be a tyrant?"

"Oh, yeah," he said excitedly. "Definitely. I remember this teacher, Mr. Barret, but we called him Mr. Parrot, be-cause he always repeated—"

"Thanks, Dad," I interrupted. "That's all I need to know. Can I be excused? I've got to a lot of homework to do."

Dad shrugged, a bit hurt. "Okay . . . but Mr. Barret was quite a character."

"Sorry, Dad," I said. "I just have stuff on my mind."

"No problem," he said, frowning like a clown. "If you need me, I'll be here . . . crying into my plate."

"As if," I said, quickly finishing my noodles. I cleared my dishes, went back into the living room, and climbed up the attic ladder, which runs up the living room wall. I lifted the hatch door with one hand, hopped onto the attic floor, and swung myself around. I turned on some music, flopped down on the small couch beside my bed, and assumed the thinking position: feet against the sloped ceiling, arms crossed on my chest, head dangling slightly over the edge of the couch.

I thought about Clouds's parting questions. Did the students at Laverton Middle School have enough power? What was the one thing I would change at school? And was I willing join Clouds in his attempt to make Acts of Dissent against Laverton Middle School?

The first question was easy. The students definitely didn't have enough power at school. We weren't allowed to decide anything, beyond what kind of food we were going to have at the class Christmas party, and even then Mrs. Topper insisted that we have fruitcake instead of choco-late. I suppose there was the student council, but a guy shouldn't have to plaster "Vote For Chris" signs all around the school just so that he can have some say about what happens during the majority of his waking life. Clouds had said teachers were tyrants, and he didn't sound that far off. We were *really* getting a bum deal.

The second question, about what part of school life I'd want to change at school, was also easy. The one thing that I found completely *unbearable* at Laverton Middle School was the weekly assembly; it hadn't changed one bit in my four years of attendance. It felt like the assembly rules were etched in stone, but as soon as I thought of it I knew it was what I *had* to change at our school.

I sighed. Somehow I needed to find a way to change the assemblies—from the Penguin's boring addresses to the painfully dull school song. It seemed like an impossible task, but that wasn't a shock. Wasn't everything impossible in my life these days?

Scanning the room for my school handbook, I found it under some old binders. I flipped through and I located the section on assemblies.

Assemblies are to celebrate the successes of the students in all facets of their education and lives.

Yeah, right. What always happened was a mind-numbing ten-minute address from the Penguin, so full of torturous pauses and repetitive statements that by the time we got to the school song the students could barely drag themselves out of their seats. The amount of eye-rolling that went on in the audience was enough to make the student council members on stage dizzy.

I closed the school handbook. It was a long shot, but it was worth trying for. I'd tell Clouds at the next meeting that I'd like to somehow change the school assembly—maybe even make it student-led—and make it fun, or at least not so yawn-inspiring.

The third answer I didn't even have to think about. I was one hundred percent in on Clouds's plan. I hadn't felt this excited in months, and I wasn't about to question it. There was something about Clouds—his infectious grin, his ready praise, and his mysterious eyes—which drew you in and made you feel good. It might sound pathetic, but no one had said I'd done something *perfect* in long time.

But I wasn't so sure how the others felt. I knew Landry was interested—it was sort of hard to miss—but I was less convinced about Boris and Susan. Clouds did seem to impress Boris, which wasn't an easy thing to do. Susan, though, was another story—she had basically everything going for her and as much to lose. So why would Susan join our group?

5

Other than a few stealthy glances at Clouds, who was working with his head down, I avoided eye contact with anyone at school the next morning. I worried that if I so much as looked at Landry he'd tailspin into one of his random babbles and spill the beans. There was no problem with Boris as he had apparently decided that if Mrs. Topper didn't appreciate his contributions, he'd just keep his head in a novel all day long. Later I saw Boris heading to the library with a chess board under his arm and a couple of seventh-grade followers at his side. During lunch, I noticed Susan hanging out with the Magnas, but quickly got myself into a snowball fight with a few classmates, so as to blend in with the crowd. The rest of the day, I just kept my head down and waited for the 3:30 bell.

When the day finally ended, I pretended to walk home but turned into Sterling Woods to wait for our meeting time. The seconds dragged as I paced between two birch trees, hidden from the road. When I finally started back in the direction of the school, my heart was racing. I ran to the school gates, peeled around the corner, and stopped dead in my tracks. Only three kids were standing at the backstop. Clouds was there, but I couldn't tell who the others were. As I got closer I saw Susan and Boris on either side of Clouds. I approached the group, and I caught Susan in the midst of a tirade.

"—And I spent all night wracking my brains about whether to come. All I could hear through it all was that blabber-brain yelling, 'I'm soooo in! I'm soooo in! I'm soooo in!' Over and over. In the middle of the night, I finally decided I would come, just to get Landry's annoying voice out of my skull. Now . . . where the *heck* is he?"

I had never seen her so worked up.

"I'm glad Landry had that effect on you," Clouds said, not answering her question with a thick-lipped smirk.

He looked at me.

"I wasn't sure you were going to come, Chris," he said. "You quiet types are always hard to read. Better to have you on my side."

"Thanks," I said, my face going red. "I just . . . I just wanted to hear what you had planned."

Susan grimaced. "I'll tell you what he has planned! He's going to ruin my future—get me kicked out of the Magnas and have me ousted from the student council. Ugh. I'm not sure this is a good idea."

"Did you tell the Magnas?" I asked, having trouble looking into her eyes.

"Tell them? Are you kidding? After Clouds came over to talk to us that first day—with his it's-a-pleasure-to-meet-you business—it would be a crime to let them know he's actually the enemy. No way. I've never seen Harriet so speechless."

Just then, a familiar lanky figure came bounding from behind the school, and raced toward us. It was Landry swinging his arms like a windmill, occasionally tripping in the snow. When he reached us he flung himself down on the ground and started making a snow angel.

"Hey folks!" he said, puffing madly. "What a crazy scramble that turned out to be! Clouds, you should have seen Terrence's face when I told him he was a slow, cross-eyed, pigeon-toed bull. I ran down Frank Street like you told me and he chased me all the way into town. I ducked in behind Al & Sal's Grocery, went through to the front and then came back like you said. He's going to kill me tomorrow."

"Thanks, Landry. Don't worry about Terrence. I'll just tell him he's still chasing minnows." He looked around at all of us. "Little does Landry know, he has saved me from my first and hopefully last mistake as leader of this group."

"Oh right," Boris said suddenly, as if he had computer wires to interface with Clouds's brain, "I saw Terrence come up to you at the beginning of the day. He was pointing at the baseball diamond—he must have seen us yesterday. Landry acted as diversion at the end of school, so that Terrence wouldn't see us again. And I guess he took the bait."

Landry sat up and smiled. "You bet. Hook, line, and sinker!"

"Nice work, Landry," Clouds said, smiling. "Terrence saw me, but didn't know who else was there. He guessed Boris and Susan—as well as ten other people—but I told him I wasn't there and that he was seeing things. Then, I got him sidetracked on another . . . project."

"I guess you saved my butt, Landry," Susan said, looking at the rest of us. "If the Magnas somehow catch wind of this group, I'm dead."

"We should get this meeting moving, then, just in case," Clouds said, pointing toward the gully, where there were still some younger students working on a fort. "Let's start with Chris and go around in a circle. What do you say, Mr. Stren?"

"Um, okay," I began. "I thought about it and we definitely don't decide enough things around here, and there are a ton of things that need changing. But the thing that bothers me the most is the school assembly."

"I *hate* the assembly," Landry whispered. "I get ants in my pants, and bored out of my skull."

"Yeah," I said, getting confident, "it is so boring. The assembly is supposed be about us, but it's not at all. The Penguin takes up most of the time with his boring speech, and there's never anything fun to it. I was thinking we could have a sort of entertainment program, where you get news reports about the cool things that are actually happening to us, inside and outside the school. There could be sports stories, skits and songs—yeah, songs we'd actually like to hear."

"What?" Landry demanded. "You aren't into 'Mighty Laverton on the River?' *Oh Lav-er-ton, Oh Lav-er-ton, the river rushing by!*"

I laughed. "Yeah, Lan, I like the school song . . . like you like detentions. Anyway, Susan's student council announcement is the only thing done by the students, and no offense, it isn't exactly, um, well, you know . . ."

I blushed and looked down.

"Don't worry, Chris," Susan said. "I know the student council minutes aren't exactly the most entertaining thing on the planet. They aren't really meant to be, but I do try to spice them up a bit. Yeah, but then Mrs. Deercroft edits everything, so that it barely sounds like my work. Um, like, hello? Do I look like I don't know how to write a few interesting sentences?"

"Hey, that was a recordable question!" Landry said, raising a finger triumphantly. "You can't fool me."

"Rhetorical," Boris intoned.

"Right, that's what I said," Landry replied with a grin.

"This is a great idea, Chris," Clouds said, smiling. "I like it a lot. It'll be challenging. But I know you'll be up for it." He looked at Landry. "What've you got for us?"

"That was *not* a rhetorical question," Landry said, smiling. "You see! I can learn stuff . . . it just takes me a bit longer. Anyway, Mrs. Topper and I aren't exactly . . . close. Right from the first day this year, she started picking on me. If it isn't because of my—okay, I'll admit it—long-winded answers, it's because of my—okay, I'll admit it again—messy desk. She always blames me for everything, but it's not like I'm always the cause of trouble. I admit that I get a little overexcited at times and I can't shut up, but it doesn't mean I'm a bad kid. She's always putting me in situations where she just knows I won't get it right, like in math period, or science, or English, or—"

"We get the point," Boris interrupted, pushing up his glasses ceremoniously. "I think it's fair to say that you deserve some of what you get, but on the other hand, maybe she *has* been treating you like the class scapegoat."

"Yeah, I'm the escapedgoat, all right," Landry agreed. "And I want Mrs. Topper to know that it doesn't feel very good."

"That sounds fair," Clouds said.

"Speaking of Mrs. Topper's class," Boris said. "I've been trying to keep my mouth shut for the last couple of days, but it's no wonder some students have trouble excelling in class when everything we learn is taught in such a boring way. We read out loud from the text, we do those stupid worksheets that are sometimes not even about what we are studying, and we take notes and listen to Mrs. Topper blab on all day long. How dry can you get? If learning is water, then Mrs. Topper's class is the Sahara Desert."

"So what's the solution?" Clouds asked.

"Well," Boris said, "there are so many cool ways to learn, beyond copying notes off the board mindlessly or being lectured at all day. I don't know how we are going to do it, but I want to change Mrs. Topper's mind about how we learn in her class."

"I couldn't agree more, Boris," Clouds said, giving the thumbs-up. "It's a great angle, and you've already warmed Mrs. Topper up to your ideas."

"Yeah, if by 'warmed up' you mean made her shoot flames from her eyeballs," Boris quipped.

Clouds laughed and turned to Susan. "How about you, Suz? What do *you* want to change?"

"Well," she said, "as I was telling you guys before, I was up all night thinking about all this stuff, but I kept on coming up to the same problem: if I join this group, I won't be able to stay in the Magnas. Leaving the Magnas would be a total mess so I couldn't even begin to think about that."

"What do you mean?" I asked.

"Well," she said, "I'm really not supposed to talk about our secrets, but believe me, it used to be a cool group to be a part of. When I was asked to be a Magna at the end of last year, I was totally honored. There is such a long history and some of the Magna alumni have gone on to do amazing things. But I'm sure all of you have noticed that Harriet and Alita have totally taken charge this year. The Magnas aren't so secret anymore, that's for sure. Or equal or respectful. That's our motto: Secret, Equal, Respectful. But now it just seems to be about popularity, and, well, power.

Boris nodded. "They are definitely behaving like tyrants."

"Yeah," Susan continued. "I thought maybe Harriet and Alita's power trip would sort of blow over, but it hasn't. It's gotten way worse, and even the other girls are getting into it. Yesterday, at break, Maria and Zigi were bored, so they teased Brenda Havelich about her new braces until she cried. Emma started *actually* pushing some seventh-grade girls the other day—and threatened to really hurt them if they told on her. Things are getting out of control. I've been trying to stay out of it, but it's kind of impossible. I'm a Magna so I always have to be with them—I'm guilty by association."

She paused for a breath, looking quite upset.

"But . . . with this group, even though we haven't really started yet, I already feel way better. It's almost like I can't refuse to be a part of this. I really want to."

"I know how you feel," Clouds said, nodding and smiling mysteriously.

"So," she continued, "what I want to do is something I could never do in the student council—I want to show the Magnas what an empty, unfair group they have become, and get them back on track. The thing is we have to be super-super-secret, or else I'm dead."

"Don't worry, Suz," Clouds said. "Mum's the word. This will be a tough Act of Dissent for you, but it's nothing you can't tackle. Which leads us to what I'd like changed in Laverton Middle School."

He paused and looked around to make sure we were all listening.

"It didn't take me long to figure out who was going to be my nemesis at my new school," Clouds began.

Landry opened his mouth to speak, but Boris put his hand in Landry's face, looked to the sky, and said in monotone, "Nemesis means the person or thing that causes your downfall. Right, Clouds?"

"Right," Clouds replied. "And can you guess who that might be?"

"The Penguin," Landry whispered.

"Right again," Clouds said. "Nice one, Lan. Very perceptive. " He turned to Susan. "The guys saw it on my first day in Mrs. Topper's class—Mr. Dorfman seriously has it in for me."

"Maybe," Boris countered, "but he's pretty rule-crazy with everybody, Clouds."

"Yeah, sure," Clouds argued, "but you didn't see what he tried to pin on me the other day when Lan and Terrence were fighting."

Landry's eyes lit up. "Yeah, I mean, really. It was just after the bell, and Clouds came over and bent down to help me, and Terrence let go right away, because he thinks Clouds is great. Anyway, all of a sudden, there was this shadow over us. It was the Penguin and he said, 'That's enough troublemaking, Mr. McFadden,' and Clouds said that he was only trying to help, and the Penguin said, 'I guess you didn't read section one hundred twenty-three'—

or whatever—'of the rules about back-talking to teachers.' And Clouds said that he did read it and that he wasn't back-talking—he was just explaining, and then the Penguin totally flipped and yelled, 'Mr. McFadden! You are seriously trying my patience. Get out of my sight before I suspend you.'"

Landry took a deep breath and looked at us excitedly.

"Yeah," Clouds jumped in, "and then I was going to remind him about the process for suspension—I've memorized that stupid rule book like a good Laverton Middle School student—but I thought I'd better keep my mouth shut."

"I'll say," Boris said. "Even *I* wouldn't be that mouthy."

"Still," Susan said. "It doesn't sound like he's being fair to Clouds. What about Landry and Terrence? If anyone was causing trouble, it was them, right?"

"Exactly," Clouds said. "And he doesn't even have the toughness to back up his rules, anyway. He just makes threats." There was a sparkle in his eyes. "So, my goal is to show Mr. Dorfman, better known as the Penguin, how stupid his rules are, and how a real leader should lead!"

"Wow," Landry said shaking his head.

"Yeah," Susan said. "Major wow."

Clouds nodded, beaming.

"Okay," Boris broke in, scratching the top of his black mop of hair. "So now we know what we want to do, but the big question still remains: How are we going to do it?"

"I've got a few plan-a-rooskis up my sleeve!" Landry said, tapping at his forehead with his index finger.

"Yeah," Susan added. "I spent all night scheming plans for the Magnas."

"The school assembly will never be the same," I said, smiling.

"And, Boris," Clouds said, "I'm sure you'll come up with some educational changes over the weekend."

Boris nodded at the challenge.

"Okay," Clouds continued, "I'm going to do some research, so that we can do this right. The important thing though is that you guys get some good thinking done. We'll meet again after the weekend, but we have to decide on a new spot to meet. One more sighting by Terrence and we're done for. I've got the school directory—I'll give each of you a call to see how your plan is coming. Enjoy your weekend—we're going to be very busy next week."

Clouds cleared his throat and gave us a warm smile. "I'm totally psyched we're going to do this, guys."

Clouds got up and walked away, and the four of us watched as he disappeared across the field.

PART 2

Revolution in the Air

6

When the phone rang on Sunday, I thought it might be Clouds.

"Hey Chris," said a familiar voice, "How's it going over there?"

"Boris?" I replied, surprised.

"Yeah. What are you doing now?" Boris demanded. "My mom's out playing bridge. Do you wanna come over?"

"I can't," I said, "I'm helping my dad in the shop today. What's going on?"

"Well, do you remember how Clouds mentioned the process for suspension from the school handbook?"

"Yeah."

"Well, I took a look and we really could be flirting with suspension or even expulsion if we join this group. On page fourteen, it says 'no gangs allowed.'"

"We aren't a gang, Boris," I argued.

"Maybe not, but in my dictionary one of the definitions says a gang is 'a group of young people who usually associate together.'"

"So . . . I guess that means you can't join the debating team this year."

"I'm serious, Chris," Boris insisted. "It says, 'no group

of students is allowed to meet without teacher supervision.'"

"Then you'd better tell your chess entourage that there'll be no more strategy sessions in the library."

There was silence on the other end of the line.

"Okay, fine," Boris said finally. "I guess you're right. I might just be a little obsessed with rules because of all the revolutionary talk."

"Yeah, sounds like it, Boris," I agreed. "I gotta go help—"

"Or maybe I need a snack," Boris interrupted. "Yeah, great idea, Chris. I was feeling a little hungry. See you Monday."

"You got it, Boris."

A couple hours later, I was sweeping in the workshop. Boris's call had me thinking about my assembly Act of Dissent again. I figured I needed to somehow get the teachers on my side before I could propose any changes, but that was not going to be easy. I swept the last bits of wood and dust into the pan, considering the ways I could get the teachers' permission, when I heard Mom calling from upstairs.

"Crick! Phone!" she hollered through the vents in the floor.

I dropped the dust in the garbage, wiped off my pants and went upstairs to the kitchen phone.

"Hello," I said.

"Chris? It's me, Clouds."

"Hey," I said, my heart rate rising instantly, "how's it going?"

"Not bad, not bad," he said. "Just thought I'd call to see how you were doing."

"I'm good," I said. "Um, yeah, I can't wait till we get started next week. I've been thinking about how I'm going to get hold of the assembly."

"Great. But don't go too far into your plans. I've been at my dad's doing some research, and I think I've got your Act of Dissent all figured out."

"Nice. Where's your dad's?" I didn't know his parents weren't together.

"He lives in the city," he said. "You should come down some time."

"Sure," I said, surprised and kind of honored at the offer.

"So, I can't wait for our next meeting either," he said, and then paused. "Speaking of the next meeting, can you think of anywhere we can have it?"

I'd totally forgotten about a meeting place. Where to do it? I didn't want to let Clouds down.

I was struck with an idea.

I replied in a whisper, "How about my place? My room is a big attic, and I've got it all to myself."

"Hmm . . . attic, eh?" he considered. "Is it private?"

"My parents couldn't hear a word if they tried!"

"Will they mind us being there?"

"I'm sure they won't," I said, but I *was* worried about having my always-concerned mother around.

"Perfect. We'll meet at four on Monday. Gotta get back to the books. See ya later, Chris."

I hung up the phone and sat down at the kitchen table. My mother, who was sorting through some newspapers in the living room, yelled out, "Who *was* that on the phone? He sounds older than you. Very lovely voice."

"Just a friend from school calling about a project," I answered, coming into the living room.

"Who?"

"His name is Clouds," I said.

"Clouds?" she said. "What a strange name. So what's this project?"

"Umm," I said, putting my hand on the ladder to my room, "it's like a special social studies group project. Mrs. Topper sort of split us into groups last week."

"Isn't that great! Sounds like a challenge for you kids," she said. "Hey, we should be getting your report card soon. Didn't your marking period end recently?"

Oh no. Report cards. I had completely forgotten about that. I knew my grades were going to disappoint her.

"Um, I don't know," I said, taking a step up. "Probably."

"With all that homework you did last term, I'm expecting some super-fantastic marks."

"I know you are, Mom," I said, climbing up a few more

steps. She sounded happy thinking about good grades, so I figured now was the time to ask. "Hey, Mom, can we have a group meeting here on Monday?"

"For school? Sure," she said, "but just so long as you are working up there and aren't just wasting time. You and Doug always used to horse around up there when you should have been studying."

"I know," I said. "It will be different—I promise."

And it was true. I already knew that this project was like nothing I had ever been a part of.

7

Before I knew it, the final school bell rang on Monday afternoon, and I was hurrying back home along Sunnydale Street, anxious to get to my house in case there were early arrivals. The day had gone by without incident, and everyone did as Clouds said: we all kept a low profile. The only thing of note was that Clouds helped some younger kids with their snow forts by the gully. It seemed a little of out of character, but by now one thing was clear to me: Clouds was full of surprises. I passed Bella's Needles & Yarn and looked into the shop. Dad was out. I grabbed the mail from the front mailbox, darted through the alley, and went up the stairs.

"Hello?" I yelled out. There was no answer.

Dad was probably out of town at the old mansion he was renovating, and my mother was in the middle of her shift at the hospital and wouldn't be home until around 8:30. I threw my bag on the sofa, got a glass of apple juice from the kitchen, and flipped through the mail.

Junk mail, junk mail, postcard for Mom, and an envelope from Laverton Middle School.

My heart sank. It had to be my report card. I stuffed

it into my bag, just as a frenzied knocking came on the back door.

Red faced and bug-eyed, Boris leaned his forehead against the door window. I got up and let him in.

"Finally!" he said in a panting whisper, throwing his bag on the floor, pulling off his boots, and sitting at the table. "Where is everyone?"

Three booming footsteps sounded on the stairs. Only Landry had both the long legs and the energy to mount the steps so efficiently. He was also panting as he let himself in and he broke into conversation like he had been talking with us for hours.

"Where's yer ma and pop?" Landry asked, hopping on the kitchen counter. "Is this where we're going to meet?" A shrug was all I could manage. "Hey, and *what* was up with Clouds today? Making snow forts? Like, that's sooo seventh grade?"

I hadn't thought of it that way. Was *Clouds* playing with minnows?

"I guess your lid had to blow eventually, Landry," Boris said. "You should have gotten a gold star for your behavior today!"

"Gee, thanks, teach," Landry said, peering out the kitchen window. "Here come Clouds and Susan."

Boris and I watched as our friends appeared, smiling, at the window. Clouds opened the door quietly and let Susan enter first.

"Great!" Clouds said, following her. "We're all here. Let's not waste any time. Chris, lead the way to your room."

They took off their boots and coats and then we made our way through the living room and up the ladder to the attic. I went up first, followed by Landry.

"Wow," Landry said, as he hopped up to the attic floor from the last step. "Cool attic. If I had this room, I'd never come down."

Susan was the next to ascend the ladder, followed by Clouds.

"This is great, Chris," Susan said, getting to her feet and looking around. "There's so much space up here."

"Yeah, it's okay, I guess," I said.

Clouds didn't say anything; he just looked around the room and nodded in appreciation. Striding over to my desk, he plopped onto my study chair, put his feet up, and looked up at the slanted ceiling. I sat on the end of my bed, and Susan, Boris, and Landry fit comfortably on my couch.

Then, in one abrupt movement, Clouds dropped his feet and swiveled in the chair. He pulled his hand through his red hair and looked at us seriously.

"Okay," he declared. "It's time to get down to business. So—"

"Um, Clouds," I interrupted. "Before we start, I need to say a couple of quick things."

"Oh, sure," Clouds said, though he seemed irritated. "No problem. That's fine. Go ahead."

"So," I said. "I told my parents that this is a school

project—a social studies thing—and I tried not to go into too many details. You don't have to worry about my dad unless you mind listening to his tedious stories. My mother, on the other hand, is a total hawk, and she's really worried about my grades." I pulled my report card from my bag and held it up. "As soon as she sees this, she's going to be all over me. So be careful when you talk to my mother, she has a way of making you say things you wished you hadn't."

"Yes," Boris said, nodding. "I am familiar with this form of motherly interrogation." He smiled. "And I don't break easily."

"Neither do I," Landry said. "I just talk too much. I mean not too too much, just kind of a lot if you know what I mean—"

"Just let me do all talking, Lan," I interrupted. "Anyway, other than that, we should always have some books and pens out when we're up here so that it looks like we're working and—"

"Perhaps Chris hasn't realized, yet," Clouds said, glaring at me, "that we *will* be working." He stopped glaring and smiled. "Just wanted to be clear out about that . . . So let's *really* get started."

Everyone scrambled for some paper and pens while Clouds began.

"Okay," he said, "as soon as I left school on Friday, I took a bus down to my dad's place in the city. It was his weekend to have me, and he had time off for once. Anyway, on Saturday afternoon, we went to his favorite café, Beatnik Brews, and so I asked him about the revolutionists in history and how they made change."

"Makin' change is easy," Landry interrupted, making his voice go like a teacher's. "If Jack has a dollar twenty-one and he buys some bubble gum for fifty-five cents, how much money does he have left?"

"Sixty-six cents, and that's not what Clouds means," said Boris. "A revolutionist is someone who takes part in forcible and complete *change of a system*, usually a government. I looked it up in the dictionary."

"Forcible. Sounds violent," Susan said warily. "I don't like the sound of that."

"Me neither, Suz," agreed Clouds. "So, anyway, he told me about some other famous leaders. Oliver Cromwell, Martin Luther King, Pinochet, Joan of Arc. The list and the stories went on and on. After two cups of hot chocolate, my mind was completely full of revolutionary figures and strategies. The next day, my dad went to work, and he said I could look over his volumes of encyclopedias and history books while he was out. After some serious research and careful consideration, I came up with five different revolutionary figures, important leaders and their movements, which can be applied to our goals at school." He opened his schoolbag and pulled out a tattered old book and a bunch of paper. "And before I left, my dad gave me copy of *Manifesto*, one of the most famous revolutionary books by that guy Marx I was telling you about." He passed it around for each of us to see. "And here," he lifted up the loose paper, "this is a revolutionary list for each of you."

After quickly glancing over the book, I passed it to Landry and took a look at my copy of the list. It was typed like the first note from Clouds and it read:

```
Revolutionary List
Landry: Nixon-1970s-Code: Get Nixon
Susan: Elizibith I-1500s-Code: Queen Rules
Boris: Gandhi-1869-1948-Code: Strike
    Peacefully
Chris: French Revolution-1700s-Code:
    People Power
Clouds: Lenon-1870-1924-Code: Topple the
    Tyrant
```

The book went around quickly without much notice, but each of us stared curiously at Clouds's list, trying hard to decipher the significance of each of the headings. We looked up at him.

"Now, let me explain," Clouds went on, "and then you can ask your questions and we can begin to plan. The list is in no particular order. The only thing for sure is that we are going to start with Landry's Code: Get Nixon and his serious situation with Mrs. Topper. The person I have chosen to represent Mrs. Topper is former U.S. President Richard Nixon. He was behaving improperly behind closed doors—just like Mrs. Topper does behind our classroom doors with Landry. Anyway, Nixon got caught. He said bad things that were recorded on tape, which made him lose his job. What we will try to do is catch Mrs. Topper on tape while she is being unfair to Landry, and then expose her."

"That won't be hard," Landry said, beginning to overheat. "We could tape it inside her desk!"

"That probably won't be necessary," Boris disagreed. "I've taped Mom's conversations from the top of my stairs."

"Creepy!" Susan winced. "What for?"

"I record her while she makes plans with friends on the phone. Hey, a guy needs to know when he can escape from his mother!"

"Please," said Susan. "I'd rather not hear the pathetic details." She looked at Clouds. "But we don't want to get Mrs. Topper fired, do we?"

"Nah," Clouds said, waving a hand, "we'll just give her a scare. Okay, so Suz, you want to get the Magnas back on track, and Elizabeth I, the queen of England, wanted to get her country back on track. But when she became Queen in 1558, she was immediately treated as an outcast and—"

"And that's who I'm trying to follow?" Susan said. "An outcast?"

"Don't worry, Suz. Eventually, the queen was able to

get the right people on her side, with convincing speeches and clever strategies. She took a poorly run country and made it the most powerful in the world. So, you will try to do the same—make the Magnas magnificent again. You need to get important members on your side so that you can overthrow them as a group and bring the Magnas back to their former glory."

"What was their former glory?" Landry asked.

"I'd tell you, Lan," Susan said, "but then I'd have to kill you."

"Susan," Boris said. "I thought you were against violence."

"Give me a break, Boris," Susan said, rolling her eyes.

Clouds laughed. "Yeah, but I'm glad to hear that attitude, Boris, because you are going to follow in the footsteps of Gandhi who was a great leader and the creator of something called 'passive resistance.' He practiced nonviolence to make positive change in India."

"Yes, I've heard of Gandhi," Boris said, nodding. "I think he did some sort of strike where he just sat and did absolutely nothing for days. Hmmm . . . I do that all the time in Mrs. Topper's class, because the work is so boring and way too easy, but it never seems to make much of a difference to her."

"Gandhi didn't just do nothing, Boris," Clouds said. "He let everyone *know* he was doing nothing."

"Hmmm," Boris said. "That sounds a little less easy."

"I'm confused," Landry said. "If I knew doing nothing

could make me famous, I would have been doing it all the time."

"The day you do nothing, Landry," Boris said, "is the day I get my nose pierced."

"Yes, Landry!" Susan said. "You can do it! And I can't wait to see the new and improved Punky Bergman."

"Don't count on it," Boris replied.

Clouds laughed and turned to me. "And Chris is going to follow the citizens of France who were trying to take power away from the tyrant King Louis the Sixteenth during the French Revolution. The peasants were starving in France, and meanwhile King Louis was always feasting on pheasant. It's the same with us. Right, Chris?"

"Um, oh yeah," I said, feeling like he was putting me on the spot—I didn't know anything about the French Revolution. "The students are sort of like . . . starving for something interesting at assembly, and the Penguin and the teachers keep feeding us the same boring assembly."

"Right," Clouds said, nodding. "So, Chris needs to write up a petition to make change, just like the French citizens did, and get it signed by the teachers. No more being shy, Chris. You have to talk to everyone about your revolutionary plan."

I couldn't help blushing as everyone looked at me.

"And finally," Clouds said, "I am going to act as one of the most famous revolutionary leaders, Lenon, who tried to bring equality to Russian people, using that guy Marx's ideas. I will try to overthrow the Penguin so that we are more equal. I want to show the Penguin how a good leader leads." Clouds beamed with determination. "Any questions?"

"When do we start?" Landry exclaimed, tapping his pen on his book.

"Soon," Clouds replied.

Boris looked concerned. "I don't like the sound of *overthrow*."

"Neither do I," Susan agreed.

"Don't worry," Clouds said, "I'm not crazy—I just want to make change at Laverton Middle School."

"Um, I don't think this is how you spell Elizabeth," Susan said.

"Who cares about spelling?" Clouds snapped. "This isn't a spelling bee, it's a revolution! Right, Lan?"

"You bet!"

"Um," Boris said, distracted. "I still have a ton of questions. Like, who *is* this Lenon guy?"

"Well," Clouds said, excitedly, "he was the leader of the Bolsh—"

The back door of our apartment creaked open.

"My dad! I'd better tell him we're here," I said, leaping off my bed toward the door in the floor.

"Oh," I added, turning to Clouds. "I almost forgot. I talked to my dad about tyrants and teachers so don't say anything about that now."

"This was all supposed to be *secret*," Clouds snapped, glaring at me.

"Sorry," I said defensively. "I don't think I said anything to tip him off."

He looked away, and there was an awkward pause.

"I really should be going, guys," Susan insisted.

"Wait," Clouds demanded, turning back. "We should probably meet here again soon. How's tomorrow?"

"I'm good," Landry said.

"Yep," Boris said.

Susan nodded.

Clouds looked at me.

"Um, yep. That works . . . I think."

"Okay, good," he said. "I want to get started on our Acts of Dissent, ASAP. Remember, secrecy is very, very important"—he glanced at me—"so keep it simple with Mr. Stren downstairs, and make sure that when you talk to other members in the group at school, you do it *inconspicuously*."

"Excuse me, Mr. McFadden?" Landry said, putting up his hand. "What does—"

"*Inconspicuously* means," Boris whispered, glaring at Landry, "not noticed, seen or heard, which for *you* means IMPOSSIBLE!"

Landry started to argue, but Clouds put his index finger to his mouth.

I opened the hatch door and yelled down. "Hey Dad, just finishing up a meeting up here. There in a sec."

We came down quietly from the attic to find Dad sitting on the couch reading the paper.

"Why so silent, folks?" Dad asked. "Hi Landry . . .
Susan . . . Boris! And who's this fella? I don't believe
we've met."

"Clouds, sir," he replied, and put out his hand to shake.
"Just moved to Laverton over Christmas. I guess everyone knows everyone in a small town. Anyway, nice place
you've got here."

"Thanks, Clouds!" Dad said, smiling. "And all of you
are right into the work already? Wow. In my day, there
was no such thing as 'group' work." I could hear his story
motor beginning to hum. "Nope, we'd just sit there and
work quietly." Susan bulged her eyes at me to say that
she had to go. "Well, we weren't always working. I can
remember one time, Gregory Thomps—"

"Dad, they've got to get going," I implored.

"Oh, right. Sure. Another time."

"Did you say Gregory Thompson?" Landry blurted out.
"He's my uncle—well actually, he's a third cousin on Dad's
side, son of John and Tonie. Tonie's a woman and she's
also my great-aunt. Wait a minute . . . I *think* she's my
great-aunt. Anyway—"

"Landry, didn't you say you were going to hockey practice?" Susan said.

"No. Hockey practice is on—"

"Landry," Clouds said, casting a spell with his intense
gray eyes.

Landry paused. He furrowed his brow. "Oh yeah . . .
Pickup hockey, you mean?"

Clouds intensified his glare.

"Oh right, right," Landry said, finally seeming to get it. "To practice my backward skating. I totally forgot. Got to get those crossovers down. Yep, practice. Gotta practice. Practice, practice, practice. Practice makes—"

Boris gave Landry a kick in the shins behind the couch. "Ow! Ow . . . I'm owwt of here!"

And before Dad could say another word, Landry fled from the room, put on his boots and coat, and was out the door.

"Well, I'm off too," Susan said. "Good to see you again, Mr. Stren."

"Me, too," said Boris. "Bye."

"Yes," agreed Clouds, addressing Dad directly. "We'll see you again tomorrow for our next meeting if it's okay with you."

"Sure, sure," Dad agreed. "Kids these days! Always got something on the go."

"So your father told me you had a meeting today," Mom said across the dinner table. "How'd it go?"

My heart skipped a beat. "Oh fine, Mom. Um . . . could you pass the potatoes?"

"That new boy, Clouds," she said, her stare penetrating, as Dad ate quietly. "Is he a responsible studier? And what about Landry? It was my understanding that he's not exactly an A student."

"Oh, Landry. He's not really a bad student. It's just that

he has a lot of energy and Mrs. Topper gives him a hard time. He's pretty eager about the project."

"And Clouds . . . ?"

"Clouds is totally into it. He was doing research all weekend." I was giving away too much information. "How was work, Mom?"

"What kind of project is this again?" she demanded. Mom changed topics like she changed opinions—never.

"Um . . . it is, like, kind of different." I should have thought this through. "It's a group study, kind of, on revolutionary figures throughout history."

"I thought you were studying Vikings this term." The woman knew way too much about my life.

"Yeah, we're doing that, too," I said. "This is an extra project on top of all that stuff."

"Seems like a lot of work to me, what with all your other subjects," she said, shaking her head. "Maybe I should call the school and—"

"Mom!" I snapped. "You promised to stay out of my schoolwork if my grades were fine . . . and they're fine."

"Well, I haven't seen any of your tests recently. And where's your report card? I'm surprised it hasn't arrived yet."

"Yeah, well," I swallowed. "Maybe the mail is just slow. So how was work, Mom?" I tried again.

"It was fine," she said. "But I'm tired. Glad I'll have the next couple of days off."

"You're off tomorrow?"

"Yes," she said. "Why?"

I looked at Dad, who I thought would say something about the meeting, but he just smiled at us.

"Oh, nothing," I said, digging into my heap of potatoes. I kept busy with my excavations, but felt her eyes on me. Mom was going to be around the next day, and I knew she was going to be trouble. I needed to make sure the group was prepared for her questions.

Later that night, I went downstairs and grabbed the "F" section of the encyclopedia. I need to get a handle on what Clouds had planned for me and Code: People Power. When I got back up to my room, I found the section on the French Revolution and lay down on my couch. Starting to read, I found I couldn't concentrate on the words—I kept on reading the first paragraph over and over, and absolutely nothing registered.

I couldn't stop worrying about Mom being around for the meeting the next day. It was too late to call the others to warn them, but I had an idea. I threw down the encyclopedia volume and went to my desk. I found a scrap of paper and wrote:

My mother will be home for our next meeting.
Watch what you say (remember: she thinks this a
school project), don't say anything about our report
cards, and try to get up to the attic as quickly as

possible. She wants to find out what we're up to.
Write your name underneath mine and pass it on.
   Chris

I folded up the note and put into my pants pocket for the next day. I got ready for bed, turned off the light, and closed my eyes. Clouds had said to be inconspicuous at school, and I really didn't want to screw up again. He seemed to get angry with me at the meeting, and it felt terrible. The last thing I wanted was to get kicked out of the group.

The next morning was a disaster, as I couldn't get the note to anyone. Clouds was recasting himself as Mr. Studious and Social, working hard in class without debating with Boris, and helping the younger students on the snow fort. He must have been planning *something*— Clouds didn't do anything without thinking about it first. Landry was still being remarkably good and quiet in class, and so at break he was like a caged animal set loose. I saw him playing soccer spastically for a bit, and then literally mid-play he bounded into a game of tag. I saw Boris going to the library with a board game called *Go* under his arm and a gaggle of his seventh-grade chess disciples trailing behind. Susan, meanwhile, was trolling the school grounds for trouble with the Magnas, but I could tell by the look on her face that her heart really wasn't in it. And me, I just wandered around, trying to keep a low profile—I'd become a pro at killing the fifteen minutes of break.

When we returned to the classroom Mrs. Topper was in her seat and she had a bunch of papers on her desk. She looked busy and flustered.

"Okay, class," she announced when everyone was seated, barely looking up from her desk, "get back to your worksheets for the next fifteen minutes."

Landry's hand went up immediately, but Mrs. Topper was engrossed her work.

He held his arm up for so long that he had to lean on his desk and prop it up with a hand.

Landry let out a big sigh, and I was sure Mrs. Topper knew his hand was raised, but she just wouldn't look up. Finally Landry couldn't stand it any longer.

"Um," he said, timidly, "Mrs. Topper . . . which worksheet?"

"Landry Colburn!" she snapped. "We don't call out in this class. And you know exactly what worksheet."

"But we did two sheets yesterday and—"

"Landry! Can you not tell that I am very busy here? It doesn't matter which worksheet. Just work and be quiet."

I saw Boris shake his head as Landry rummaged nervously in his desk. He finally found a crumpled sheet, shrugged his shoulders, and got down to work.

Shortly before lunchtime I was given permission to go to the restroom. I was feeling stressed about the impending note hand-off and figured some cold water to the face would snap me out of it. Just before I turned into the boys' room, however, I saw Susan walking toward the office. I whistled softly through my teeth to catch her attention. When she turned, I hurried toward her and pulled the note from my pocket.

"Hey," I whispered.

"What's up?" she replied, nervously glancing up and down the corridor.

"Just a bit of a problem. Take this and pass it on ASAP," I breathed, and then turned toward the restroom.

My heart dropped when I looked down the hall.

Standing twenty feet away, her mouth gaping open, was Sherry from my class. She must have left the room right after me. If Susan was seen as one of the nicest members of the Magnas, Sherry was definitely one of the meanest. In class, she was always the first to laugh when someone got something wrong, or to jump on a piece of gossip and spread it around. On the other hand, she really knew how to suck up to Mrs. Topper, who seemed to blindly adore her.

I looked down at my feet in panic and rushed into the boys' room. I could smell Sherry's perfume as she hurried towards Susan. Safe in the restroom, I checked under the stall doors to see if anyone was there. There was no one. I paced back and forth. I stopped in front of a sink to catch my breath, and caught my pale reflection in the mirror. There was no doubt about it: we were busted.

I didn't go back to class until after the lunch bell rang. Mrs. Topper cast me a suspicious glance as I grabbed my lunch and my coat, but she was busy with students on lunch detention, and didn't speak to me. I wasn't sure whether I should rush outside or hide in the library, but ended up in the schoolyard. It didn't take me long to see the uproar I had started.

The Magnas were huddled together at the center of the basketball court. They surrounded Susan and were firing questions at her from all sides. Susan stood answering questions calmly. Sherry spotted me on the steps and pointed, which incited a flurry of giggles. I didn't know what to do. My heart was in my throat.

I turned and went back into the school. I walked up the corridor and to our classroom, where Mrs. Topper was eating her lunch, watching over her detention students.

"Um, Mrs. Topper?" I said. "I'm feeling a bit sick. Can I put my head down on my desk?"

"Sure, Chris," she said, like this explained why I'd been in the washroom so long. "That's fine."

I went to my seat and put my head down, but my heart was still racing like mad.

When the 3:30 bell finally rang, I rushed out of class and jogged home. I found a note on our kitchen table. It was from Mom saying that she'd gone out with a friend and would be back around four. I waited anxiously in the kitchen, until I heard Landry's few, loud steps up the stairs. He knocked and then came in.

"Hey, partner, what's going down?" he said, kicking off his boots. It didn't appear he knew what had happened.

"Did you get the note?" I asked.

"Yeah, yeah. I won't say a word. My lips are sealed. My teeth are locked. My tongue is in a state of suspended animation."

I relaxed a little and said, "Then why am I still worried?"

"It's in your nature," he said, holding his chin like a scientist considering a theory. "You are a natural worrier. *Un worrier naturel.* A real worrywart. A wart of worry—"

We heard slow footsteps on the back stairs. My stomach tightened. Susan's auburn head appeared in the window followed by her beet red face. I readied myself for the worst and went to the door.

"Hi," I said as I opened it.

"Are we ever in a lot of trouble," Susan said as she took off her shoes and coat and fell onto one of the kitchen chairs. "I feel like I've been through the Spanish Inquisition."

"What happened?"

"What the heck're you two talking about?" Landry demanded. "I have that 'I'm going to get a detention' feeling."

"Well," Susan began. "You know that note I passed to you, Landry?"

"Yeah, that was weird," he said. "You were with Sherry.

What did you say? 'Could you give this note to Chris' or something?'"

"What?" I exclaimed. "We're ruined. I'm doomed." I lifted my hands to my head. "Sorry. I screwed up again. I'm so—"

"Don't worry, dude! I passed it on to Boris," Landry said.

"But—"

"Hold on a second, will you?" Susan insisted, looking at both of us. "It's not what you think. Let me explain."

But before she could start we heard a group of voices coming down the alley. We sat silently as Clouds, Boris, and *my mother* came up the stairs and entered the house.

"Why so quiet, kids?" my mother said, kicking off her shoes and putting her purse on the counter. "I've just had a very good conversation with your friends. Sounds like the project is really getting under way." She beamed affectionately at the two boys, especially Clouds. "They tell me that you'll need to get right down to work. An hour is hardly going to be enough time. Right, Clouds?" She gave him a wink and a warm smile, and then spoke to us all. "I'll get you some snacks while you get settled in."

"Sherry knows about the group!" Landry whispered to Boris and Clouds after my mother had delivered the milk and cookies.

"What?" Boris said, ripping himself from his thoughts.

"Sherry Linton! Oh my gosh! That girl is trouble. She beat me up in second grade, and I still haven't recovered."

Clouds didn't flinch and turned to Susan, who was still rubbing her temples. "Care to explain, Suz?"

She looked up, shrugged, and then glanced at me.

Clouds also looked over at me, and my stomach dropped.

"Um," Susan said, saving me from his lethal stare. "It's not as bad as you think. I guess I'd better explain."

She recounted the tragic occurrence in the hallway, starting with when I whistled to her. Boris slowly shook his head as she continued. Landry listened like a kid at story time eating a cookie and lying on his chest with his feet kicked up behind his head. Clouds sat at my desk chair looking only slightly concerned. But when Sherry's name came up again, not even Clouds could hold back from wincing.

"Sherry," he said, leaning back in the chair and putting his hands through his red mop, which was growing unruly. "You mean the Magna in our class with short black hair."

Susan nodded silently.

"I've been watching her in class," Clouds said, looking at me critically. "Not the kind of person we want as an enemy."

"Believe me," Boris added, and grabbed a cookie. "She is probably the worst adversary we could have."

I needed more details. "So how bad is it, Susan?"

"Well," she continued, not looking directly at me. "After you took off to the boys' room and left me helpless, Sherry charged over and said, 'What's the note say? Why'd he have that guilty look on his face? What's going on behind our backs?'"

She took a deep breath, and then continued. "I had to think quickly so the first thing that came to my mind"—she then looked over at me with a strange expression—"was that you were asking me out on a date."

"What?" I blurted out, feeling suddenly hot and claustrophobic in my attic. There was silence as they watched my face turn from white to red.

"Sorry, Chris," she said, "but it was the only way I could distract her from the truth. I knew that anything guy-related would, like, immediately get her on the wrong track. I also knew that I could claim the note as personal so that she could not demand to see it. There's a rule from something we sort of follow called the Magna Charter. By the time I got out for lunch, Sherry was an ally for us, telling the girls how you passed a note to ask me out and how cute that was."

"Oh, please!" Boris demanded. "Spare me the soap opera."

"Anyway," she continued, ignoring Boris. "The . . . um . . . Revolutionists are still together, which is the important thing." She looked at Clouds and me for support.

Landry was still confused. "But what about when you came over to *me* with the note and said, 'Give this note to

Chris,' and then winked and mouthed, *Pass to Boris*."

Boris jumped in. "Use your head, nitwit! Susan had to get Chris's message to everyone. So she got it to you so that the rest of us could find out about Mrs. Stren's snooping. But a better question, Lan, is what did Susan tell the Magnas was in her reply note?"

Susan looked at the floor timidly. "What could I do? The girls all think Chris would be the nice, romantic type."

Boris and Landry groaned, as I blushed.

"So," she said, looking over at me. "I told them I was accepting his invitation."

"Chris and Suz are going on a date!" Landry bellowed. "Now *that* is funny!"

Clouds glared at him and pointed below. Landry dipped his head submissively but kept grinning. Clouds cleared his throat.

"That was an excellent bit of thinking, Suz. You saved Chris . . . and the Revolutionists—love that name, by the way!—and you two can figure out the details later on." He seemed restless. "We need to get into some serious planning of our first operation, Code: Get Nixon. Get out your pens and paper."

We scrambled around for our stuff, and Clouds began.

"Landry and I talked on the phone last night, and we've come up with a plan. President Nixon was the thirty-seventh president of the United States starting in 1969, and he wasn't such a great leader. First of all, when he became president, he took money away from the poor. Kind of like Robin Hood, but in reverse."

"You mean he went into their houses and took their stuff?" Landry asked. He apparently hadn't been paying attention during research time.

"No," Susan interjected. "Sometimes leaders take money away from social programs like welfare that support poorer people."

"Right," Clouds agreed. "He also slowed down racial equality."

"Yes, that sounds familiar," Boris agreed. "The 1960s were an important time of change for equality for African-Americans."

Clouds nodded. "So Nixon was against these positive changes and all of those who were for it. So, he put bugs—you know, little microphones—in his enemies' buildings so that he could find out their secrets and political plans. In the end, though, it was *his* conversations that got him in trouble. He always recorded his own discussions and these tapes were used as evidence against him when he was arrested."

"If he was so bad," I said, needing to forget about the date with Susan and me, "how was he elected in the first place?"

"Well, first of all, he was persistent," Clouds explained patiently. "He'd been running for president for years before he got elected. Also, he traded favors to powerful businessmen for money and support, which was illegal and was one of the things that was found on his tapes and almost got him kicked out as President."

"He almost got kicked out?" Landry asked. "I didn't know they could do that."

"It's called impeachment," Boris stated. "I saw a TV program on Nixon. I think he quit before he was impeached."

"Well, I don't know if I want to *impeach* Mrs. Topper!" Landry said. "I just don't want to be picked on."

"Right on, Lan," agreed Clouds. "All we want to do is give her a bit of a scare so she realizes how she's treating you. Now let's figure out how we're going to get that tape close enough to her so that it comes out clearly."

"Hey, Boris," Susan said, thinking. "How big is this tape recorder?"

"About half the size of a chalk eraser. Why?"

"Do you think it could fit in Landry's shirt pocket over there?"

Landry was wearing his plaid button-down shirt, the only kind of shirt I could ever remember him wearing.

"Sure, so long as the pocket is loose and not buttoned up," Susan said, leaning over to him and flapping his open pocket, making Landry squirm away.

"Wouldn't it fall out easily then?" I inquired.

"Not if he doesn't move around too much," Susan said.

We all gave Landry a skeptical look.

"What? I can do it!" Landry declared, throwing his

arms in the air and nearly hitting Susan in the face. "Slow and steady—that's me. Cool as a cucumber. Smooth—"

"We know you can do it, Lan," Clouds interrupted. "We know you *will* do it." He paused. "Now, Boris, you'll have to get the tape recorder to Landry tomorrow. When can you do it? It'll have to be a safer pass than the Sherry Linton incident." He gave me a forgiving wink.

"I can do it in the morning," Boris answered. "At our lockers like Lan did with Chris's note. We're right near each other. That way he'll have all day to record."

"Hey, speaking of Chris's note, how'd you get it, Clouds?" Landry asked.

Clouds smiled at Boris. "He could have just passed it back to me, but Boris was careful. Remember when he passed out the school notices, and how he happened to drop them right around my desk and ask for my help?"

Boris's eyes grew behind his lenses. "Not bad, eh?"

"Yeah, not bad!" I agreed. "And, hey, what did you say to my mother? I've never seen her so gushy."

And to that, Clouds only grinned.

After the meeting, Mom was busy making dinner.

"Did you get a lot done?" She turned to me, her hands covered in bread crumbs.

"Yep," I said. "They're a really good group to work with."

"Clouds and Boris were just delightful. And that Susan—she's such a pretty girl."

"Yeah, I guess," I said, trying to avoid the subject. "Mom, I'm going to be up in my room. Okay?"

"Sure," she said. "We're fifteen minutes away from eating."

When I got up to the attic, I flopped on the couch and assumed the position: feet up, arms crossed, head back. I let out a big sigh. It felt like things were spinning out of control. I was suddenly going out on a date, or something like it, with Susan, one of the most popular girls in school. We were ramping up to perform our first Act of Dissent on Mrs. Topper, which was going to be tough and risky. Suddenly Boris's worries about suspension didn't seem so crazy. On top of that, I felt like I was walking on eggshells with Clouds. My life had gone from seriously boring to downright bananas. It was thrilling, but a bit scary, too.

I reached down to the floor for the "F" encyclopedia volume to finally start my research, but I found my open bag instead. I felt around for my Revolutionist sheets, but instead my fingers grasped an envelope.

I'd completely forgotten. My unopened report card. I held it up to my attic light, wincing to see if I could see through it. No luck.

I thought for a moment. If I opened the report card now, it would look like I'd been hiding it, and there was no doubt in my mind that this report card would mean trouble. In September, I'd lucked out on a couple of early tests, and showed them off so that Mom would get off my back. After that I kept on opening my books to study when I was supposed to, but I just couldn't concentrate or even care, and my grades began to show it. Short of an administrative error or a downright miracle, this report card was going to be seriously bad. At best I was looking at a three-way meeting between Mrs. Topper, Mom, and me. Still, I knew that if the report didn't show itself soon, Mom would call the school, and things could get worse.

"Chris! Dinner's on!" Mom called out from below. "And bring down your homework for after dinner."

I got up with the report card still in hand and slung my book bag over my shoulder. I walked to the hatch door and opened it. I took a step down, and then another. Just as my head was level with the floor, I looked at the report card and sighed. I placed the envelope on the floor and slid it back into the room.

9

Landry sat in the class the next morning with a slight bulge in his shirt pocket and a smug look on his face. I looked back at Clouds and Boris, who were serious and heads-down. Landry had clearly given up on trying to please our teacher. Throughout the morning, he asked a few long-winded questions, and you could tell that Mrs. Topper was irritated even before he finished. At morning break and at lunch, I saw Landry racing out to the snowy field, and I worried that he still had the recorder in his pocket. I tried to catch Cloud's eye for a wink, a smile, anything, but the seventh graders' snow fort appeared to be getting a new addition, and he was completely in charge. Clouds wasn't playing with minnows, he was ordering them around.

After lunch, the bulge in Landry's pocket was still there, and I crossed my fingers that the recorder still worked. Mrs. Topper, who is always more cranky after a strenuous morning, looked tired when we took a math quiz. She looked even crankier when Landry knocked his pencil case off his desk, creating a clattering cacophony.

"You did that on purpose, didn't you?" she accused.

"No, I just," Landry replied, ". . . you said we needed to use a pencil so I—"

"I said that fifteen minutes ago and the quiz is over!"

"Yeah, but I just remembered I had a really short chewed-up one in my pencil case, and since I didn't answer all the questions I thought I could use it for them. And then I was digging in my case when—"

"Landry!" she snapped, her face burning. "Stop wasting our time. Just give me the answer to the next question."

"Um . . . didn't understand that one."

"What kind of answer is that?" she demanded. "If you would just listen for once, you might get it right. Never paying attention. Never!"

Landry shrugged.

"What's so funny?" she demanded.

"Nothing. I just—"

"Wipe that smile off your face and pick up your pencil case."

"Okay, but I wasn't—"

"Enough, Mr. Colburn. I'll see you after class."

Right after the final bell, I stopped at my locker and saw Magnas Sherry, Zigi, and Emma looking my way. I hadn't seen Susan all day, and I didn't need any convincing that this was my cue to get lost, quickly. I grabbed my books, turned to go, and almost ran right into Doug and Zach.

"Hey," Doug said. "How's it going, man?"

"Um," I said, looking beyond them and desperately wanting to escape. "Not bad."

"What have you been up to these days?"

I looked back at the Magnas, who were watching me even more intently.

"Um, not much," I said. "Same old, same old."

"Really?" he said, looking over at the Magnas. "That's not what I heard . . . You asked Susan on a date."

"Oh, yeah . . . that," I said. "I guess I did."

"Nice one, dude," Zach said, nodding.

"Yeah," Doug said, punching me lightly on the shoulder. "Totally didn't see that coming. Impressive."

"Yeah," I said, feeling stuck. "Thanks. Look I gotta go, guys—my dad needs some help in the shop."

"Sure, no problem," Doug said, walking off with Zach. "We should hang some time."

I watched the guys until their backs were turned and then sped away.

I'd only been home for a few minutes when the phone rang.

"Hello?"

"Hi Chris, it's Susan!"

I muttered a pathetic "Oh . . . um . . . hi."

"I had student council stuff at break and lunch," she said. "How did the beginning of Code: Get Nixon go today?"

"Um . . . I think well," I said, feeling suddenly light-headed.

"Great," she said.

There was an awkward pause.

"So listen," she said. "The Magnas were asking if you had, like, responded to my note and I told them I was hoping you'd call tonight. So I thought I better, um, call so that, well . . . I could tell them you did. "

There was a pause for me to speak, but *nothing* was coming out.

"So . . . what do you think?" she asked.

"Well," I said, straining to come up with the words, "yeah, I guess we should . . . I mean I'd like to . . . it's no big deal . . . we'll just, you know, go out somewhere."

"Where?"

"Ummm . . . how about Alfredo's?"

Where did *that* come from? The Italian family restaurant in town wasn't exactly party central.

"Alfredo's?" she said, giggling. "The Magnas will love that. They guessed you'd be a real gentleman . . . and a romantic."

I *really* didn't know what to say.

"So when?" she asked.

"Um . . . Friday?"

"Sounds good," she said. "For the good of the Revolutionists, right?"

"Yeah. Sure. For the good of the Revolutionists."

"So," she said. "I'm also calling to tell you what to do tomorrow. Clouds phoned last night with a plan."

"He did?"

"Yep."

"What do I have to do?"

"That's just it," she said. "You're off the hook—nothing. Just keep your eyes off of the other Revolutionists in class."

"What's happening?" I said. "What are we doing?"

"I guess Boris will splice the tape tonight," she said. "And I have to go to the—"

I heard talking in the background.

"I gotta go," she said suddenly. "If we don't get a chance to chat I'll see you at six on Friday at Alfredo's. Okay?"

"Um, okay, but—"

"Oh my gosh," she interrupted. "I almost forgot. We're meeting tomorrow at three forty-five in Sterling Woods, fifty feet in from the Happy Holiday Motel sign. Do you know where I mean?"

"Sure, but—"

"Apparently there's a big maple tree right there. Got to go," she said. "My mom needs help. Bye."

"Bye," I said, and hung up the phone.

I scratched my head. Why wasn't I called about the plan? Was Clouds still mad about the whole telling-my-dad-about-tyrants thing? For the next twelve hours it was all I thought, dreamed, and worried about. The suspense was killing me. What was Clouds up to?

Nothing happened before break the next day, and I did as Susan told me—I kept my eyes down when I was around the other guys, especially with Clouds. When we came back from break, we were just settling into a lesson when the PA system clicked in. It was an unusual time for an announcement, so the class went silent. Then I noticed Boris wasn't in class.

The announcement began with a nasally, high-pitched voice.

"*Is this how your teacher should treat the students at your school?*"

Then it was Mrs. Topper's and Landry's voices. "*What kind of answer is that? If you would just listen for once, you might get it right. Never paying attention. Never! . . . What's so funny?*"

"*Nothing. I just—*"

"*Wipe that smile off your face and pick up your pencil case.*"

"*Okay, but I wasn't—*"

"*Enough, Mr. Colburn. I'll see you after class.*"

While she listened, Mrs. Topper's face went red, then redder, and then a deathly deep purple. She glared at Landry. "What are you up to?"

"Why do you always blame me?" Landry cried.

Sally Walder put up her hand.

"Yes, Sally?"

"Was that announced to the whole school?"

Mrs. Topper's eyes bulged. "Oh my . . ." And then she rushed to the door, just as Boris opened it from the corridor. He wore his usual disinterested frown.

"Where have you been?" she demanded.

"Getting the school notices, like I always do."

"Well get to your seat. And class, the math work is on the board."

When she left the room, the room erupted in conversation. The Magnas huddled around Sherry, and a few students rushed over to Landry, who they assumed was responsible. Boris and Clouds played it cool, staying in their seats, while Landry just kept shrugging and claiming his complete innocence. The clamor continued for at least five minutes until Mrs. Topper returned to the room. The class went silent, and the students hurried back to their seats.

We watched in silence as she walked to her desk. Sitting down carefully, she straightened her books for moment and then stared at the back wall. The silence was so intolerable that several students got down to their work. I couldn't—I was mesmerized. Our teacher said almost nothing for the rest of the day, and only left her seat once to put more math exercises on the board.

One thing was clear: the Revolutionists had taught Mrs. Topper a lesson. But why didn't I know how they'd done it?

10

What an incredible caper," Landry burst out. "A splendiferous prank. Did you see the look on her face?"

We were standing in shin-high snow in Sterling Woods.

"Yes! Excellently executed, people!" Clouds said, leaning against the big maple.

"What happened?" I said.

"Chris, sorry, man," he said. "I decided to get things going with Code: Get Nixon, and I tried to use the skills that were needed. The way it worked, the best thing for you to do was be safe and quiet . . . which you're good at."

"I guess," I said, trying not to look offended.

"So, let's explain it to Chris," Clouds said. "Suz, how'd it all go down?"

"Well, when I saw Boris pass our classroom, I waited for three minutes like you said, Clouds, then I excused myself to get our notices at the office. It was deserted so I guessed Boris had been successful in getting Mrs. DeSantis to leave the office. I know how the PA system works because of the student council announcements I have to do. I slapped in the tape, punched in room 5—and *only* room 5, so that the rest of the school wouldn't hear—and pressed Play. It was a pretty nerve-wracking thirty seconds, I can tell you that much."

"Yer not kidding," Landry gasped.

"Yeah, well, as soon as it was over, I whipped the tape out and hurried back to class. When I got there, my classmates were as quiet as ever. They hadn't heard a thing." She let out a big sigh. "How'd the tape sound?" She directed this question at me with a smile.

"Clear as a bell," I replied. "Whose voice was that with Landry's and Mrs. Topper's?"

"So it worked!" Boris exclaimed, jumping in. "Thanks, Chris. It took about thirty recordings to make my voice unrecognizable. Still, it wasn't as hard as convincing Mrs. DeSantis that there was a suspicious salesman outside in the parking lot. She wanted to know everything about this guy before she'd even budge. What did he say to me? What was he selling? How tall was he? Where did he go? Why did he just talk to me? Jeez, I thought I had every detail covered, but that woman is a bona fide Sherlock Holmes!"

"There was a salesman outside?" Landry said. "What was he selling?"

"Duh, Landry," Boris groaned, smacking his forehead. "Ever heard of a diversion? You know, after all this, I feel like maybe I have *some* sympathy for Mrs. Topper."

"What'd Mrs. Topper do after she heard the tape?" Susan asked.

Clouds, who was still leaning against a tree, finally stepped forward. His eyes were like ice. "It looked like she was going to strangle Landry, before Sally so innocently asked, 'Did the whole school hear that?' It was perfect. It was *better* than perfect! Then," he said, swallowing, "Mrs. Topper left the classroom. I bet she went to find the Penguin to try to explain. I can just imagine the crazy conversation they would've had. Once Mrs. Topper realized that the Penguin hadn't heard the announcement, she was probably speechless, scared . . . and seriously confused." He grinned. "Serves her right."

"I don't know," I said. "Mrs. Topper looked pretty shaken up. I kind of felt sorry for her."

I guess I was also upset about being left out of Code: Get Nixon.

Clouds glared at me, and a shiver went down my spine.

Then, like the flick of a switch, Clouds smiled. "Don't let it get to you, Chris. We did the right thing. I know—it's hard when you aren't involved. We'll get you in the mix next time around."

"Sure," I said, suddenly not wanting Clouds—or any of them—to question my dedication to the Revolutionists. "I guess you're right."

"Hey, now," Landry said, raising an imaginary mug in the air. "It's time to celebrate, not question. Let's hear it for our first Act of Dissent—to my escape from being an escapegoat or whatever it's called."

We all laughed, raised our fists and bumped them in the air.

"Excellent work, troops," Clouds declared.

"Hey," Landry suddenly realized. "You never told us what your mysterious task was in Code: Get Nixon."

"Well," he said, "along with organizing you guys, I was just lying low like Chris. We don't want to be exposed all at once. That way if someone goes down, the rest of us can continue on."

"Goes down?" Susan said. "That doesn't sound pleasant."

"It's not going to happen, Suz," Clouds said confidently. "Hey Chris, do you think we can meet at your place again on Monday?"

"Um, yeah. Sure," I said, feeling like it was all I had to offer.

"Great, and don't worry, buddy," he said, winking at me. "You're going to get thrown into some crazy stuff sooner or later."

"Okay," I said, smiling. It seemed impossible to stay angry at Clouds McFadden for long.

"No meeting today, eh?" Mom said at dinnertime. "I thought you guys were going full steam ahead."

"Yeah, well," I hesitated, trying to say it right. "We, like, all have our own parts to research now. So we're taking, um, a bit of a break."

Dad ate silently.

"Oh, really?" she asked. Conversations like this were like harmless, mountain-peak snowflakes that transformed suddenly into catastrophic avalanches. "And what's your focus of research?"

"Ummmm . . . the French Revolution and stuff."

"The French Revolution?" she said, her eyes wide. "I studied that in college. What about it?"

"It's kind of like . . . a drama . . . a dramatization like on TV . . . of the signing of that charter thing."

"The Declaration of the Rights of Man and of the Citizen? Wow! That's pretty heavy for eighth grade. Are you su—"

"Mom," I snapped. "Thanks for the interest, but it's going just fine."

She paused for a moment to scoop a forkful of stir-fry, but she wasn't done prying.

"By the way," I said, bracing myself with a wince, "I'm going out with Susan Miranda tomorrow for dinner—at Alfredo's."

Dad's jaw dropped.

"Susan? How exciting!" Mom exclaimed, and her sudden buttery smile was like nothing I'd ever seen before. "Wow, wow, wow. Dinner with Susan Miranda. If our Christopher hasn't grown up already." She reached over like she was going to pinch my cheek, but I moved my head out of the way.

"Mom! It's no big deal. We're just friends." I could feel my face heating up, so I stared down at my plate. "It's no big deal."

"Yeah, honey," Dad said to Mom. "I remember my first date and, well, let me tell you, it was no big deal. It was one big *disaster*!"

"We know, John," Mom said. "And we've heard that story one too many times."

"No we haven't," I said. "What happened again?"

"Well," he said, leaning back and looking at the ceiling. "It's funny you should ask—"

"Please, John," she warned.

"Yes, please," I pleaded. "Let's hear it, Dad. Wasn't it Hillary Ham?"

Dad smiled and continued to tell the outrageous story of his first date with Hillary, which included a car accident, a slip in a mud puddle, and a vigorous slap to Dad's face. Mom tried to stop him with her paralyzing stare, but Dad's eyes were stuck on the ceiling, and they would not return back down to us until he had finished his saga.

When Dad finished, I didn't give Mom a chance.

"Can I go do some work in my room?"

"Sure, Crick," Mom said, distracted, looking at Dad like she had some words for him.

Back in my room, I picked the "F" encyclopedia off the attic floor. I needed to prove to Clouds that I was Revolutionist-worthy. It seemed like I couldn't do anything right these days—or I just wasn't being included.

I went to my desk, sat down, and started to read about the French Revolution. I went through the first section once without taking notes, and then read again with a pen in hand. After an hour, I looked down at my scribbled notes and sighed. Mom was right—the French Revolution was heavy stuff. I read through the section one more time. I had to get this right.

· PART 3 ·
A Steep Cliff

11

Sorry I'm late," Susan said, walking into Alfredo's. "I was over at my grandma's place and the time got away."

"That's okay," I said. I had only been waiting at the table for a few minutes, and I had taken the opportunity to try to get my heart rate down. "Your grandma's? Do you always visit her?"

"Well, not always," she said, putting her mittens and hat in the arm of her coat, and hanging it on the back of her chair. "Because I have other responsibilities like schoolwork and stuff, I see her less. It's hard, though. My grandma and I are like two peas in a pod."

"Huh," I said. "I've never heard of anyone being *friends* with her grandma." I only had one living grandparent. Grandpa Mel lived in Florida, and I only saw him at Christmas at my aunt's and uncle's. "What do you talk about?"

"Well, everything—school, the Magnas, even though I'm not supposed to, and of course, boys," she said, smiling when she said the last part, and not seeming the least bit embarrassed. I fiddled nervously with my fork as she considered her next thought. "She also knows about Clouds and the Revolutionists."

"Really?" I said. "Are you serious? What does she think? Does she agree with what we're doing? Would she ever tell your parents?"

"First of all, she never tells me what to do—she's not my mother after all—and she would never tell on me. She's my friend, and like any good friend, she lets me know what she thinks without intruding."

"What do you mean, without intruding?"

"Well, for example, whenever I mention Clouds she rolls her eyes or puts her hand to her brow and says, 'Oh dear!' But she never says anything more than that."

"So I guess she doesn't like him then."

"I wouldn't actually say that. Maybe she's a little suspicious or something. She sure did think Code: Get Nixon was risky." Susan looked seriously out the window for moment. "She also said something else that I've been thinking about."

"What?"

"She said that we should watch ourselves, that history must not be repeated."

"What did she mean by that?"

"I don't know," Susan said, shrugging. "I guess we moved on to other things . . . like this date. She thinks it's cute."

The word "date" hit me like punch.

"Do you know what you want to eat?" I asked in a frenzy, trying not to look at her brown eyes.

"Yep," she said, giggling into her menu.

What was she giggling about?

We were both silent as we studied the menus. When the waiter arrived, Susan ordered the spaghetti and I asked for the pepperoni pizza. By then, I'd regained my composure and was able to change the direction of the conversation.

"Umm . . . so how'd you think Code: Get Nixon went?" I asked.

"I thought it went well," Susan beamed. "It was scary, that's for sure, but we'll have to see if Landry gets treated better in class."

"Yeah, I guess," I said.

"It wasn't very nice of Clouds to exclude you."

"He didn't exclude me," I said, defensively. "He was just using the different skills of the group."

"I don't know," she argued. "Harriet does that all the time, not letting me know something is going on, to, like, have some sort of power over me. It's like she's intimidated by me or something."

"Well that's not what happened with Clouds," I snapped.

Susan smiled. "So there is a little fight in you, Christopher Stren?"

"Yeah," I said. "Of course there is, and don't call me Christopher."

"Sorry," she said.

"Um . . . me, too," I said. "I shouldn't have snapped like that."

"Yes, you should have," she said. "You have to stick up for yourself sometimes, *Chris*."

I wanted to say that I did, but I wasn't so sure. I looked away and thought for a moment.

"Anyway," she said. "Forget it. You're probably right. Clouds was just being a good leader, using the skills that were needed." She smiled. "So, how are the plans for Code: People Power?"

"Well," I said. "I've been doing some research, and I think I kind of get it. The Third Estate was this group that represented the people in France, and it wanted to give people all these rights and freedoms, which they definitely didn't have at the time. All the common people or peasants were starving and King Louis the Sixteenth was living large in this castle called Versailles—he really didn't want to give up his power. This other guy the Marquis de Lafayette was elected to this thing called Estates General, and then, um, I think it was on July 11, 1789, Lafayette presented a declaration of rights resolution that he'd written. And then a new draft was made, and that got the ball rolling. So, I think that's who I'm going to follow: Lafayette. I need to write a resolution that demands control of the school assembly. I'll get all the teachers to sign it."

"Cool!" Susan said. "It sounds like you totally get the French Revolution stuff."

"Yeah, I guess I do," I said, smiling. "What about Code: Elizabeth Rules?"

"Well," she said, "back in the 1500s, Queen Elizabeth

would have had your head sliced off for taking her power away. Or maybe even worse. She might have had each of your legs and arms tied to ropes attached to four horses, and then she would have sent them galloping in different directions."

"Yikes," I said, crossing my arms tightly. "A woman could have had someone torn apart in the 1500s, but meanwhile, she barely had any rights two hundred years later in France."

"But Elizabeth wasn't just a woman, Chris," she said, her eyes flickering. "She was the Queen. A powerful and crafty queen."

"Oh," I said.

Susan looked like she was thinking.

"So," she said, "I'm pretty freaked about taking on the Magnas."

"You are?" It was hard to imagine Susan scared of anything.

"Yeah," she said, "Harriet is totally out of control, with Alita as second-in-charge, and they seem to have the rest of the Magnas under an evil spell." She forced a smile. "I've got the Threes Cs targeted as my most hopeful allies, but it's not like I've said anything to them yet. I feel like they'd turn on me in a second if I did."

The Three Cs—Catia, Carina, and Christine—were all in Susan's class and they were inseparable.

"Man," I said. "I wouldn't want your job."

"Who're you calling 'Man'?" she snapped jokingly.

"You'd better watch your language around this woman or she'll have you beheaded! Queen Susan, Ruler of Laverton." She threw up her nose regally, and laughed, her eyes sparkling.

"Well, ye Queen," I said, feeling brave, "what are you going to report to the Magnas about this recent occasion?"

"Well," she said, with the thoughtfulness of someone truly powerful. "I don't know," she said in her real voice, and gazed out at the snowy street for a moment.

"Got it!" she said, finally, upright again like Queen Elizabeth and imitating a British accent. "I decree three reasons why we should report this dinner a grand success. First, if we say that this meeting was acceptable, we can keep the Magnas busy with nonsense and gossip while I scheme my Act of Dissent. Second, this, um, relationship will allow us to converse regarding the Revolutionists and our plans without raising suspicion in front of everyone at school. And last, but certainly not least, I'm kind of having fun!" For the final part, she lost the accent again and blushed a little.

The waiter approached with our plates.

I picked up the accent with a little less skill, and bowed.

"Your wish is my command."

12

"Hey, there fellow Revolutionist!" Clouds barked to me on the phone on Saturday. "Long time no talk."

"Hey," I said, surprised that Clouds was calling *me*. "Um, how're things going?"

I was at my desk, and I had just finished the first draft of my Act of Dissent resolution.

"Great," he said. "We haven't checked in for a while. How goes your research?"

"Umm . . . pretty well, actually," I said, confidently. "I'm just putting the finishing touches on my resolution. Want to hear it?"

"Sure. Go for it."

I read out the piece, enunciating each word carefully.

> To All the Teachers,
>
> A group of eighth graders at Laverton Middle School feel that the students should run part of the school assembly. If students are able to contribute to this weekly event, we will definitely make it more interesting, more student-focused, and more fun. It is only fair that we, as representatives of the student body, have some influence on the

celebration that is really supposed to be for and about us.

If you agree with this, please sign here:

Thank You,

The Revolutionists

"Yeah, great," he said, sounding a bit distracted. "Listen, pal, I need a favor."

He seemed nervous all of a sudden.

"Sure," I said. "What's up?"

"Um, I kind of need a place to stay tonight because . . . because Mom and I got in a big fight because, well, she was just being *totally* unreasonable. Anyway, I said I was going to go to my dad's but when I called him he said he was busy with work, but then I sort of stretched the truth with my mom and told her that my dad said it was okay to come down to the city. I don't usually ask for favors like this . . . I just feel like I can trust you, Chris."

Something told me not to pry, and I was just relieved to finally have an opportunity to prove my worth to a real revolutionary leader. "No problem. I'll see if it's okay."

Mom was at the hospital, so Dad's permission would have to do. I opened the hatch door, and stuck my head down.

"Dad! Can Clouds stay over tonight?"

"Fine with me," he yelled from the kitchen.

I returned to the phone.

"Sounds good," I told him. "My couch is your couch."

"Awesome," he said, sounding relieved. "I appreciate it, man."

"So when are you coming?"

"I've got a few things to do. I'll be there before dinner," he said. "Hey, Chris?"

"Yeah?"

"I owe you, big time."

When Clouds knocked at the back door in the late afternoon, Dad and I were glued to a football game on TV. By the confident look in his clear, gray eyes, Clouds was feeling back in charge.

"Watching the game?" he asked, and then dipped into the living room to greet Dad. "Good afternoon, Mr. Stren! Who's winning?"

"Oh," Dad said. "It's a tie, 21–21."

Clouds shook his head. "Never understood why someone would want to *play* football. The coach is the one with all the power. He controls everything. That's who I'd want to be."

My father smiled back, but he was distracted by the game. "Good to see you, again, Clouds. Have a seat and watch if you like."

Clouds glanced over at me and raised his eyebrows.

"We're gonna go upstairs," I said.

"Okay, boys," Dad said. "Have fun."

When we got up to the attic, Clouds said, "Hey, thanks again for having me, Chris. I knew you'd understand."

"Yeah," I said, even though I'd never come close finding myself in the position that he was in. "So . . . you got in a big fight with your mom?"

"Yeah," he said, "she's worse than the Penguin with all her stupid rules—but I never follow them. Speaking of my mom, can I use your phone for a sec? I need to tell her"—he smirked—"I've arrived at my dad's."

"Won't she somehow know you're here?" I said, pointing him to the phone by the desk.

"No way," he said, smiling. "She's seriously low-tech. We don't even have an answering machine."

He dialed the number and waited. When his mom answered, I could hear her loud but distorted hello on the other end of the line.

"Hi Mom. I'm here," Clouds said, winking at me.

I listened as his mom talked for a least a minute.

"Yeah, sure," Clouds said, smirking. "No problem."

Then, his mother's voice got even louder like she was yelling at him.

"Yes, Mom," he kept on saying, and then she asked a question. There was silence, and then she asked it again.

Clouds smiled weakly and turned away from me on the couch, and his voice went soft. "Yeah, of course . . . I've already done it. . . . Yes, when I get back tomorrow . . . I promise. . . . I'll show you all of my work tomorrow. . . . I told you I promise. . . . Um, you too . . . I said . . . you too. Bye."

There was an awkward silence.

"Wow," I said. "Sounds like you were getting an earful."

"Yeah," he said, rolling his eyes. "But I set her straight."

"Yeah, right," I said. I thought he was being sarcastic, but I could tell by his glare that he wasn't.

"I *don't* follow my mother's rules, Chris," he insisted.

I shrugged and looked away. From what I heard of their conversation he wasn't exactly rebelling.

Clouds leaned forward. "Let's be clear, okay?" he said, pointing a finger at me. "When it comes to my mom, and everyone, *I'm* in control. All the time."

"Right, sure," I said, not wanting to ruin our night.

"So," he said, suddenly cheery. "How'd your date with Susan go?"

"Um," I said, startled by the question. "Well, um, it wasn't really a date. We just had dinner."

"So what happened after? Did you kiss her?"

"Um, no," I said, blushing. "I just . . . just walked her home. I mean . . . the only reason we went out was to protect the Revolutionists, right?"

"Sure, sure," he said, smirking. "I understand. Girls are intimidating to some guys. . . . So why don't we take a look at that assembly resolution you've been working on? It sounded a little too uptight and formal. I think it needs a little dash of revolution."

"Um, sure," I said, feeling thrown off-kilter by his erratic swings in conversation.

I grabbed the resolution from my desk, scanning it as I returned to the couch. "By the way, I'm sort of following this guy Lafayette's life. He was important during the French Revolution and he was the main author for the Declaration of the Rights of Man and of the Citizen, which was this resolution that—"

"Don't worry," Clouds said, snatching the sheet from me. "I'm way ahead of you. I know all about Lafayette." He waved me back over to my desk. "Now it's time to make this resolution sing."

The meal with my parents and Clouds was a lot less difficult than I'd thought. Mom was tired after her day at the hospital, and Dad was his usual jovial self. When Dad wasn't going on endlessly, Clouds was charming my mother with his own stories. He told all kinds of tales about the Revolutionists—he didn't call us that—which made us seem like the most dedicated, resourceful, and interesting students around. My mother occasionally looked at me in disbelief as Clouds told stories of my successes at school.

The next morning, Clouds said he had to get home right away without breakfast. It was really cold out so I lent him a hat, which he pulled over his thick red hair. Before he left, he winked and said, "Let's keep the fact that I stayed here between me and you. Okay?"

"Sure," I replied. "Mum's the word."

After he left, I helped Dad in his workshop, and then we joined Mom for brunch in the dining room. I was thinking about Clouds's up-and-down behavior the night before when Mom asked, "So how'd it go with S—?"

"Just fine, hun," Dad said, not looking up from his seat. "Chris was just helping me cut some two-by-fours and—"

"No, John," she said, "I was asking Chris how his date was! We haven't had a chance to ask him about it."

"Oh right," he said, hitting his forehead, and looking over at me. "Your date. So, how'd it go?"

"It was fine," I said.

"Fine?" Mom said. "What did you do?"

"We ate . . . and talked," I said.

"What did you talk about?"

"MOM!" I said.

"I was just asking!" she said, putting up her hands.

We ate silently for a bit.

"Chris," she said, solemnly. "With all this *date* excitement and Clouds staying over, I forgot about your report card. I wanted you to know that if it doesn't come on Monday I'm going to have to call the school."

"But—"

"No buts," she said firmly. "Irene Maitland said her Martin got his last week."

"Fine," I said. A bad report card would mean more homework, more prying, and way less freedom. I wasn't prepared to give that up just when the Revolutionists were hitting their stride.

13

I nearly choked when Boris walked into class on Monday. He'd shaved his hair so that there was only black stubble peppering his oversized skull. Instead of the usual large, Coke-bottle glasses, Boris wore tiny spectacles with thick lenses. He wasn't hunched over in his normal antisocial gait but walked slowly and deliberately with soft footsteps. In assembly, I heard Landry call out, "It's Boris the Buddist," which had Mrs. Topper's eyes blazing and the rest of the auditorium in stitches. Our teacher scolded Landry, but he didn't get a detention. Ever since Code: Get Nixon, Mrs. Topper was much less strict with him.

At morning break, Boris sat alone in one corner of the field on this woolen mat in the snow with his legs crossed and his arms resting on his legs. On the other side of the school grounds, I saw Clouds having a heated discussion with the Penguin by the snow forts, and I was willing to bet it was about our principal's favorite subject: the school rules. On the basketball court, the Magnas were scattered in various conversations, and Susan and Sherry were whispering to each other. What was she up to?

Then after break, during our social studies lesson, I

glanced back and saw that Boris wasn't copying down any notes. Mrs. Topper didn't seem to notice—maybe she was just trying to survive the day without another disaster.

After I had lunch, I finally made contact with a Revolutionist: Susan walked right up to me in the schoolyard.

"Hi there," she said casually.

"Should we be talking?" I said, glancing toward the Magnas. Harriet, Alita, Emma, and Zigi were looking right at us.

"Yes, definitely," she said, laughing like I'd just said something funny. "If we didn't, then they'd get *really* suspicious. What the heck is up with Boris? Did he get a lobotomy? That's definitely not what I had in mind for Punky Bergman."

"Yeah, what a nutbar," I said, shaking my head. "I guess he's taking Code: Strike Peacefully pretty seriously. I'm sure we'll get the full Bergman report at the meeting this afternoon."

I saw Clouds peer out from one of the snow forts and stare at us for a couple of seconds. I smiled at him, but he'd already turned away. I was thinking of saying something to Susan about Clouds's staying over the weekend, but remembered that I'd sworn an oath of silence. The conversation we had in my room about his mother had stuck in my mind. Why didn't he want to admit that he followed his mom's rules?

Then Susan leaned close toward me, touched my arm

and half-whispered, "I should go back to the girls. They'll die from wanting to know what I'm whispering to you right now."

"Um, sure," I said, laughing nervously.

"See ya, cutie," she said, smiling like she really meant it.

Cutie? How could such harmless a word make me feel like both throwing up and throwing my arms up in celebration?

After school, I ambled alone along Sunnydale, still slightly dazed by my short but sweet conversation with Susan. When I arrived home, Boris was already at the top of the steps, sitting cross-legged. He looked down at me peacefully.

"Hello, Chris," he said.

"What's with the head, man?"

"I shaved it."

"I can see that," I said. "What about the glasses?"

"My grandfather's," he said. "The prescription is remarkably close to mine."

I shook my head, and before I could ask another question I heard voices in the alley. Susan came around the corner with Clouds. She grinned at me, and I smiled back. I felt a twinge of jealousy that they'd arrived together.

"Hello, fellow Revolutionists," Clouds said, grinning as he came up the stairs. I couldn't help smiling back.

We heard two more voices in heated in discussion echoing from the alley. I listened carefully. It was the worst possible situation: Landry and my mother were having a *conversation*.

"Landry," I called out desperately as they turned the corner.

Landry wouldn't stop, and Mom wasn't stopping him.

". . . So, like, we're kind of doing a show, like a demonstration thingy, with Acts of Distaste, for the class. It's a five-act show, like Shakespeare, you know. Yeah, like Shakespeare. It's—"

"Landry!" I repeated, so as to stop his talking.

"—an epic play with drama and revolution!!"

"Landry!" I yelled so loudly, that both Landry and my mother looked up in astonishment.

"What is the problem, Christopher?" Mom demanded. "There's no need to raise your voice like that. Landry was just trying to explain what your project is about. I must say I am getting a little confused. I didn't realize you were also studying Shakespeare."

"No, no, Mom—Landry's just pulling your leg. He likes to joke around, don't ya, Lan? A great storyteller, isn't that what Mrs. Topper always says?"

"Well, yeah, sort of," he said as they both climbed to the top of the stairs, and we all stepped inside, taking off our boots and coats.

"Yes," said Clouds. "Landry is an exaggerator. But it's also true, Mrs. Stren, that he's our creative genius. Whenever we need to brainstorm, Landry is simply the best."

Landry looked confused, but honored.

"But what are you actually doing for this project again?" Mom said.

"Ahem!" Boris piped in. "I know this all must be confusing for you."

"Boris!" Mom said, putting her hands to her face. "I didn't recognize you. You . . . you cut your hair."

"That's an understatement," Landry said, giggling.

"Yes," Boris said, going a bit red. "I was tired of the, um, old look."

"You weren't the only one," Landry said. "But haven't you gone a little far with the whole Code: Strike Pea—"

"Anyway," Boris almost shouted, stepping in front of Landry and looking at Mom. "About our schoolwork: Mrs. Topper has started a new independent project where the students determine their own goals and topics of interest."

I watched as the doubt fell from my mother's face.

"We have chosen revolutionary figures as our topic," Boris continued, "and we now have to come up with a way of presenting our information. We spent the last week doing some research so we will be able to discuss what we will do today." He paused with emphasis. "I'm sure Chris would be glad to explain what we've come up with once we have finished our meeting."

I nodded, but felt less than assured.

"Shall we?" Clouds gestured toward my attic ladder. "Time to get to work."

My mother smiled at me, convinced for the time being that all was okay with my education.

We climbed up the ladder and settled ourselves in our regular seats.

"So, what's up with the head, cue ball?" Landry said, leaning over and rubbing Boris's hairless cranium. "What'd ya do, join the army or somethin'?"

"Quite the opposite, my friend," Boris replied, though not in his usual peevish tone. "Under the guidance of the Great Soul, Mahatma Gandhi, I act peacefully. With no army."

"Um, hello?" Susan said, pretending to knock on Boris's head. "Is there anybody in there? I think we're losing you, Boris! What's the deal?"

Boris grinned knowingly. "The deal is that I have a new understanding of the world through Satyagraha: truth, determination, and nonviolence." He put his hands up together at his chin. "Just as Gandhi tried to free India from the shackles of Great Britain's tyrannical government, I will release the students from boring lessons and useless worksheets. I made my first passive act against Mrs. Topper today."

"You sure did!" I agreed. "But I wouldn't call shaving my head like Gandhi and meditating in the field very passive. More like strangely active!"

"Not that, you idiot—I mean, my friend!" The old Boris was fighting to get out, but the Gandhi in him regained composure. "I didn't take down notes for that lesson on the Vikings. Copying notes is no way of learning anything."

"Great show, Boris-baby!" Landry said, his sarcasm teasing. "You could tell the class was completely amazed by your first Act."

"Change is sometimes gradual, Landry," Boris said, still calm. "Let me explain about Gandhi so that you'll understand a bit better."

"Will it help explain why you look like a yoga teacher?" Susan said, giggling.

"I'm not even going to answer that question," Boris began. "So . . . at first, Gandhi was a lawyer in South Africa where he tried to get all these human rights for Indian South Africans. Then he went back to India, his homeland. He struggled for years against the English government, which kind of owned India at the time.

"The way he wanted to make change was totally different from other leaders. He believed in this interesting idea called Satyagraha, which combines the virtues of truth, determination, and nonviolence. I'm trying to do my Act of Dissent with all these three things in mind."

"Didn't he, like, starve himself or something?" Susan joked, giving Boris a pinch to his gut.

"Hey, hands off the property! Nonviolence, please!" he said, rubbing his tummy. "Yeah, he did. Just by stopping eating, he made people think differently!" Boris rubbed his chin and reconsidered. "But if I stopped eating, Mom would freak. Mom's version of Satyagraha is food, food, and more food. She really believes in the stuff."

"This is really great, Boris," Clouds said. "I love it. You're like, what do they call it . . . a method actor, really getting into your role. Nice. But I bet you have something *else* cooked up."

"Maybe something with curry and chickpeas in it?" Landry said with a smirk.

Boris bit his lip so as not to react to Landry. "Yes," he nodded to Clouds. "Next time, I'm going to *announce* my Act of Dissent and ask anyone in the class to join me."

"Wicked!" Clouds exclaimed.

"Sounds like a plan," I agreed.

Susan frowned. "Sounds like trouble."

"What's life without a little trouble?" Clouds asked, grinning mischievously. "What about you, Suz? What's up with Queen Elizabeth?"

"Well, I haven't had much chance to do research for Code: Elizabeth Rules with all of my student council work. But from what I've read, two things have sort of stuck in my mind. One is that she chose not to marry so that she could avoid war."

"What do you mean?" I asked.

"Well," she said, smiling at me, "back in the 1500s, all the European countries like France, Spain, and England were always attacking each other over land, power, and even religion. But at the same time, the kings and queens from the same countries were marrying each other. Weird, huh? Like, the prince of France would marry the queen of Spain! Hello? Are you totally insane? So anyway, Elizabeth didn't get married and she pretended to be interested in other countries' royal men so that they wouldn't attack England."

"Nice move, Beth-baby!" Landry said, giving a thumbs-up.

"Excellent political maneuvering," Clouds agreed.

"I agree," Susan said. "I'm not really sure how *that's* going to help with me and the Magnas, but the queen's speaking skills definitely will. She used her powers of persuasion to get what she wanted from her government."

"And you will do the same with the Magnas?" Boris asked skeptically. "Good luck!"

"Boris, a little peaceful support would be nice," she said, nudging him.

Then she leaned forward and lowered her voice. "Okay, I do have a plan but you can't tell anyone anything—it has to be even more secret than the Revolutionists, because I'm seriously breaking the Magna code of silence here. I would die of shame if other *good* members . . . and past members—" she pointed toward the trap door and mouthed "*Chris's mom*—knew I was doing this."

"Mrs. Stren is a Magna?" Landry yelped.

"Former Magna, Landry," Susan whispered with her finger to her mouth. "And I said it's a secret! Why do I suddenly feel like Mrs. Topper?"

"Oops," Landry said. "Sorry."

"It's okay," Susan said. "So, there this thing called the Magna Charter, which is like our, well, our rule book." She turned to Clouds. "There's only one copy and it is given to a current Magna to keep safe. And yeah, guess who has it?"

"Harriet," Clouds said, like he already knew.

"Right, but it doesn't really matter because no one ever looks at it," she said. "Here's the thing though. The important Magna rules were told to us in June, and every Magna has to know them by heart. Anyway, one of the rules is that each Magna is acting leader for a month. The leadership doesn't really matter that much, it's just sort of representative, but one of the responsibilities is that the leader must be present at all meetings. And that's the thing about the Magnas—or at least how we used to be—we are all equal. No one has power over anyone else."

"That's what Lenon wanted," Clouds said excitedly.

"Well, there's wanting it, and then actually getting it," Susan said, grimacing. "No one has really paid attention to the monthly leadership rule since Harriet and Alita took over, because they are basically tyrants bossing us around. But we did do a schedule last June and I wrote it down. January is Sherry's month to be acting leader, and after that it's Harriet's." She winced. "So I have no choice. I've got to get Sherry on my side."

"You can't be serious!" said Boris in his real voice.

"Make sure she doesn't punch you in the arm five times—it hurts."

"Won't she be hard to convince?" I asked, remembering their whispering in the schoolyard.

"Well, maybe," Susan replied, "but my grandma told me that sometimes the people that act the meanest are actually the ones who, deep down, are really insecure. They're just scared to open themselves up. Because of the whole thing that happened with Chris and me"—she averted her eyes when she said this—"and the note, and, um, stuff, Sherry and I have been talking more often. I said a couple of things to her about how mean Harriet and Alita have been, and she looked at me and nodded sort of cautiously, so I'm pretty sure she agrees. She's only going to be official leader of the group until the end of January so I need to get her on my side soon. And then hopefully from there, I can get *all* of them under my thumb in no time."

"Sounds like you've got some work ahead of you, Suz!" Clouds said, sitting up. "Now as for Landry, because Code: Get Nixon has been completed, I've asked him to be my second in command. I will occasionally need someone to be my voice and my legs." He winked over at our lanky, long-winded friend. "And Landry is exceptional in both of these departments."

"Yeah," Landry said, nodding. "We're, like, working on an escape route from the snow forts to the back door and—"

Clouds froze Landry with a stare.

"Let's keep focused," Clouds said to him, and then looked at me. "What about you, Chris? How goes Code: People Power?"

"Good," I said, grabbing the resolution from my bag and then looking around at everyone. "Clouds and I worked hard on this resolution together"—Clouds's eyes flashed and widened reminding me that he didn't want me to say anything about him staying over—"um . . . on the phone . . . the other day. And . . . this is what we came up with."

Clouds nodded, and I read it out.

To All the Teachers,

A freethinking group of eighth graders at Laverton Middle School insist that the school assembly be run by the People (the Students). If school citizens are in charge of the assembly, they will make it more interesting, more student-focused, and way more fun. It is only fair that the students have control of this weekly celebration. It is really for them.

If you agree with these statements, please sign below:

Power to the People,

The Revolutionists

"Should we really put 'Power to the People' and 'The Revolutionists' in?" Susan asked. "The language is pretty strong. It might make them suspicious."

"I think it'll make us sound more serious and revolutionary," I said, repeating Clouds's words from the weekend.

"I'm not sure I consider myself that kind of revolutionist anymore," said Boris, sounding like Gandhi again.

"Whatever, Mr. Meditation!" Landry sneered.

"Listen, Landry," Susan said seriously. "Chris is going to have to go straight to the teachers with this, and I've done that sort of thing before. It isn't easy. It's got to be as teacher-friendly as possible."

"Okay, fine, we'll have a vote," Clouds declared. "All those in favor of the Assembly Resolution as it is, 'Power to the People' and all, raise their right hand."

Landry's hand shot up like a rocket.

Clouds lifted his arm.

I looked at Susan, and then at Boris. It appeared as though they were waiting for *me* to decide. Three of five would make a majority.

I suddenly felt unsure.

I looked at Clouds, who glared at me.

"Um, well, it's my piece of work," I said with a shrug. "So I guess I'm for it."

My arm went up, and Susan's head dropped.

"Fine," she said to the floor. "But you'll see."

"Right, then, that's decided," Clouds said abruptly. "Let's move on. Chris, you start passing it to some teachers. We need signatures from all of them if we want to convince the Penguin to give us that assembly."

I nodded, but felt like Clouds was rushing by my Act of Dissent. I hadn't explained about Lafayette yet.

"In the meantime," Clouds continued, slowing his speech deliberately to bring everyone back to him, "there's my own Act of Dissent. I am going to take the Penguin and his stupid rules *down*."

"Yeah," Landry jumped in. "You should have seen Clouds at the snow forts the other day. The Penguin was saying, 'Blah, blah, blah, school rules,' and Clouds said, 'It doesn't say "no fort building" or "no snowballs" in the handbook!' The Penguin narrowed his beady little eyes at Clouds, and said to all the seventh graders that could hear, 'Kids, you'll know who to blame when I make some new amendments to the school rules!'"

"Yes," Clouds said, nodding proudly, "and like Lenon in Russia, I will rally the People and revolt against this tyrant and his idiotic rules. And I will need the help and support of *all* the Revolutionists, if I am to succeed."

Susan shrugged but didn't argue.

"About that Lenon guy," Boris queried. "I couldn't find him on the Internet. I kept on getting this weird, long-haired guy named John Lennon who was really into peace. How do you spell this guy's name?"

"Like I put in our list," Clouds said, with irritation. "Anyway, we've got to wrap this meeting up. Anyone have any questions?"

"No," Susan said. "I gotta go."

After an awkward silence, the meeting adjourned. Mom wasn't around when we got down, so it was a quick, uneventful good-bye.

When they were gone, I fell back on the door, a terrible feeling coming over me. Susan was mad at me, I was sure, and Clouds had gotten really worked up about my resolution and the vote. He didn't even let me speak about my own Act of Dissent, and I was getting tired of being pushed around. It felt like things were changing with the Revolutionists, and I wasn't sure if it was for the good.

My eyes fell on a pile of mail on the kitchen table. I stared at it for a moment in a thoughtful daze. Then I felt the blood rise to my face as I remembered: my report card! The time was now. I would be way worse off if Mom actually called the school like she'd threatened. I flew through the living room, up my ladder, and grabbed the envelope from my desk drawer.

When I got back to the kitchen, I shuffled through the mail. There were two big pieces of junk mail, between which I decided to stick the report. I looked at the envelope. It was postmarked a week earlier. I slid the report card in and arranged the mail so it looked like it had before. If I was lucky, Mom wouldn't look through the mail that night, before she started a new shift. If I was lucky, she wouldn't notice the postmark. *If* I was lucky.

14

I was lucky. The mail stayed untouched on the kitchen table all night, and Mom was gone when I came down for breakfast. Dad is always a little out of it in the morning, so I escaped with not much more than a wave and a smile. When I got to class, I had my resolution in my back pocket. Mrs. Topper had a board full of notes for us to copy down about Vikings' home life. She told us all to start writing while she did some of her own work at her desk. There were several groans from the class, but everyone eventually got out their social studies notebooks and began taking down the notes.

Everyone except Boris.

He stood up calmly. "Excuse me, Mrs. Topper, may I say something?" He asked it politely, *almost* respectfully.

"Yes?" Mrs. Topper said, confused by his new tone.

Boris shoved his thin spectacles up the bridge of his nose and crossed his arms. "The history of the Vikings is very exciting and interesting, but it is my opinion that copying down notes from the board is possibly the most boring way to learn this subject. I propose—"

"Excuse me?"

"Forgive me, really, I don't mean to be rude, Mrs. Topper, but don't you think that some student research on Vikings would be more effective way of learning this information? I mean, we *do* have a library, and we could break into groups or simply work as individuals. We could choose the specific topics we are interested in, and then could teach others what we've learn—"

"Boris!" Mrs. Topper interrupted. "Sit down and stop wasting our time. We have already determined that my twenty years of teaching experience trumps your ZERO days. End of discussion."

Boris's face turned red, but he didn't budge. He looked down for a moment and then raised his chin.

"You leave me no choice, Mrs. Topper," he said. "As a passive revolt against this form of teaching I am officially going on note-taking strike. I invite anyone in the class who agrees to join me."

Boris sat down at his desk, put his pen ceremoniously in his pencil case, zipped the case shut, and laid his head gently, face down, on his desk. There were a few giggles, but no one else moved.

Terrence, seizing any opportunity to cause trouble, immediately piped in, "Yeah! I hate note-taking."

He slapped his pen heavily on his desk—as he had no pencil case to put it in—and put his head down with a clonk.

Now no one giggled, but several students shifted nervously in their seats. Mrs. Topper, who was turning red, raised her eyes to the ceiling. When she returned her gaze to the class, the redness had reached her eyes: they were flaming torches.

"Boris Bergman and Terrence Fripp, you can take these notes down now or at morning break. The rest of you get writing, please."

Terrence lifted his head and tried to catch Boris's eye, but Boris's forehead was still rigidly placed on his desk. The rest of us got down to our note-taking. After about five minutes, Terrence let out a big sigh and began writing furiously to catch up. Terrence *lived* for break.

Boris did not move until the bell rang, and even then he only lifted his head, looked at Mrs. Topper, and put his head back down.

When I stepped out of the school, I was hoping to go talk to Susan, but she was involved with the Magnas and I didn't want to get in the way of her strategy. Sherry was talking to the whole group, and it looked like she was acting out what Boris had done, because she was wearing Catia's glasses and crossing her arms like our bald-headed friend. On the other side of the grounds, Sally Walder had a small audience of do-gooders in front of her, and my guess was she was relaying word for word what Boris had done in our class that morning. I caught the tail end of Clouds disappearing into the completed snow fort complex, with Landry and a gaggle of younger kids in tow.

The teacher on duty was the strict but nearsighted Mr. Singh, and the Penguin was nowhere to be seen. For now, the forts appeared safe from rule amendments. I stepped toward Mr. Singh, thinking he could be the first one to sign the resolution, when I saw Doug running my way.

"Hey, Chris," he said. "Wanna play tackle soccer in the snow?"

This was a surprise. Maybe hanging out with Susan had raised my coolness quotient. I looked at Mr. Singh and decided not to approach him—he would be a too-tough sell after my disaster grades last year.

"Sure, I guess," I said, and ran out to the field.

I returned to class tired and wet to the bone. Boris still had his head on his desk, and Clouds was acting as if his be-spectacled friend did not exist. When math class started, Boris quietly opened his books to participate again. He answered questions only when asked, but when he did, his tone was friendly and unfazed. When our science class on space started with notes again, Boris methodically put his stuff away and assumed the same head-down position.

Mrs. Topper was clearly frustrated that Boris was insisting on continuing this strange behavior, but she had nothing left to punish him with beyond sending him to the Penguin, which she wasn't going to do after Code: Get Nixon. Boris kept his head down, and Mrs. Topper didn't bother him. When the lunch bell rang, Boris got up to go, and I noticed Mrs. Topper didn't flinch. Perhaps she was hoping that letting Boris off would make the whole note-taking strike just go away.

Outside, Landry ran toward me in a wild-eyed tizzy, but it was because he was being chased by a couple of younger students. I noticed that Boris's chess pals had caught his crazy bug, and were now meditation mates—they had surrounded him in a cross-legged circle, each with their own blanket to sit on, in the far corner of the field. I didn't see Susan or Clouds anywhere outside, which made me nervous. I went to the snow forts and couldn't find Clouds. I knew I wasn't supposed to connect myself to him and the other Revolutionists, but I was tired of following orders. I asked a few seventh graders if they'd seen Clouds around and everyone shrugged. I walked around every inch of the school grounds and peered up the empty hallway of the school. Where could they be?

When lunch ended, I trudged back to class. There was a sheet on each desk—it was a special school notice. I heard several students groan, and I looked up to see the disastrous effects of Boris's revolt etched in white chalk on every inch of the blackboard. I'd never seen a board so full of words, notes, arrows, diagrams, and equations. It was like Mrs. Topper had taken all of the knowledge about space and the universe, and crammed it into one small black galaxy in front of us. Even Sally could not hold back a shoulder-sinking sigh.

Terrence and several other boys stared at Boris fiercely, and I thought I heard Sherry hiss at him. I stuffed the notice in my desk and continued to watch people's reactions.

"You'll pay for this," Terrence said, loud enough for everyone to hear. Clouds slipped into class quietly, just before Mrs. Topper. I tried to catch his eye, but it was impossible.

When Mrs. Topper finally strode into the classroom, she had a self-satisfied look on her face. She put some books on her desk and then turned to the class.

"All right, everyone! Get your science notebooks out. You've got some serious work ahead of you."

There were more groans.

"Now, before we begin," Mrs. Topper said, raising her voice, "I'd like you all to know that you can thank Boris for your lesson today. Start copying what's on the board, and I don't want to hear a word out of any of you."

Almost everyone gave Boris dirty looks, but he wasn't paying attention. Clouds was whispering in his ear and jabbing his finger at the school notices. What was getting Clouds so excited? I opened my desk to grab the notice when Mrs. Topper cleared her throat.

"Boris, Clouds, what part of 'not a word' didn't you understand?"

I closed my desk and watched. Clouds stopped whispering and opened his notebook. Boris sighed, stood up, and spoke.

"I am sorry to say," Boris spoke carefully, "that I now have two reasons for an act of unaggressive dissent. Not only has our teacher decided to give us more notes, but she has also acted with revenge against a student in her class. Unfortunately, her retaliation will affect every single student here. As a revolt against note-taking and vengeful attacks on innocent students, I will not take part in this lesson." He paused and looked around the room. "I ask anyone who feels the same to join me in this peaceful action."

There was a silence so powerful that I winced. The students around me turned their eyes to Mrs. Topper, who'd begun nervously tapping her pen on the desk, keeping her eyes fixed on Boris.

Boris sat down and returned her gaze confidently.

Landry did an eerie Western whistle, which got only a couple of quiet giggles given the severity of the situation.

And then there was another strange sound.

It was the sound of pencil cases opening, pencils being put away, books closing, books being tucked away in desks and heads dropping down on desktops. It wasn't methodical, like dominoes falling in a row, but it was happening. Some students were doing it independently; others needed encouraging looks from friends and desk neighbors. I saw Magnas Zigi, Emma, Sherry, and Maria whispering back and forth, weighing their options. Landry was the first Revolutionist to stop work, after about ten other students had quit. I waited until at least half the class had lowered their heads, and then slowly put my stuff away. I turned my head to the side as I dropped, and I saw that Clouds was also getting ready to descend. Within a couple of minutes, there was only one student still working: the devoted Sally.

Before we knew it, the bell rang to end the day. When I went to my locker, there was a serious buzz in the hallway. I looked at Boris, who seemed to be in his own revolutionary world. Landry was talking to a few guys from our class, unable to contain his excitement. Clouds wasn't at his locker and I couldn't see him anywhere. I looked down the hall toward Susan's locker, but she wasn't around either.

When I got to Dad's shop, I checked the empty mailbox and then peered in through the window. Dad was sweeping, so I knocked on the window. His eyes lit up, and he waved for me to come in. The ring of the overhead bell heralded my entrance.

"Crick," he said. "Guess what I found today?"

"I give up."

"Your report card," he said. "It must have come a couple of days ago. We haven't been on top of the mail these days."

"Oh, great," I mumbled.

Dad smiled knowingly. "Not expecting the best report?"

"Not really," I said, shrugging.

"Well," he said. "I didn't open it. I remember what it

was like to get my report card, and I figured you might want a little time with it before your mother gets home."

I nodded and sighed. "Thanks, Dad," I said, patting him on the arm as I walked by. "I'll remember this."

"No problem," he said, calling after me. "Just take care of me when I'm old and arthritic."

I ran up to the house, grabbed the report card off the kitchen table, and went up to my room. I threw my bag down and assumed the position on the couch. I held the envelope up and then ripped it open. I unfolded the report and took a deep breath.

"So I hear your report card finally arrived," Mom said, at the dinner table.

"Yep," I said.

"How is it?"

I reached into my pocket and dropped the folded report on the table between us.

She opened it up, and her face fell. She looked at her food and then at Dad. There was a painful silence.

"Christopher," she scolded. "Cs and Ds are not even close to good enough, and you know it. I'm going to see Mrs. Topper as soon as possible, and until we figure out this mess, you are grounded. Home right after school and no phone calls at night . . . unless you've got a good explanation."

"Um, well, I just," I said, scrambling mentally. "Just . . ."

"That's what I thought," she said. "After dinner bring down your *homework*."

"Fine," I said, and slowly ate the rest of my meal, but I was really getting tired of everyone telling me what to do.

15

Mrs. Topper didn't give me an opportunity to brood about my grounding the next morning.

"Class, everyone quiet and in your seats," she said sternly. "I have something important to say."

The class quieted down.

"I've always thought I was an honest, fair, and reasonable teacher," she said, "and I *assumed* that over the last *twenty years* I had learned something about teaching. But Mr. Bergman says he wants to learn differently, and he's received some support from you, class. Therefore, I am willing to try to do things differently."

Boris couldn't help smiling. It was all happening so easily.

"Perhaps," she said, over some surprised mumbling from the class, "there is a better way of learning these topics. I'm putting it in your hands. Everyone take out a piece of paper and on one side write 'Vikings' as a heading and on the other side write 'Space.' Work on your own, or work in groups. I want you to brainstorm as many ideas as possible about how we could learn this material. Any questions?" She looked around at the startled class. "All right, begin."

I'd never seen the class work as hard as they did that morning. Students were brainstorming, arguing, constructing, conniving, planning, and thinking. Some groups wrote mind maps, and others drew illustrations. Ideas were flying everywhere and most of them were landing on paper. Not once did Mrs. Topper have to get out of her seat to keep students on task. Actually, Boris filled in as teacher, wandering around to different groups and individuals and encouraging people with appreciative praise and enthusiasm. It was the first time I'd seen all of the students in the class, even Terrence, get into their work.

The enthusiasm lasted all morning long. At break time, I stepped out the school doors, and was surprised when Susan suddenly was standing right in front of me.

"How've you been?" Susan asked. "Feels like we haven't talked in ages." Her hair was tucked into a green winter hat, which made her brown eyes lighter.

"Not bad," I said, wanting to ask her where she'd been yesterday. "Yeah, things have been so crazy these days with Boris's thing and stuff." Something felt wrong. "So, what's going on?"

About half the Magnas passed us silently.

"We have to talk, Chris," she said, eyeing the girls. "We . . . um . . . can't go out on any more dates and talk like this. Okay? It's hard to explain right now, but you have to trust me. I just can't tell you right now. Things won't be different with the Revolutionists, you know . . . Sorry." She looked at me hard. "Understand?"

"Fine," I said coldly. "Your wish is my command."

"Why'd you have to say that, Chris?" she snapped. "I thought you of all people would *trust* me."

I shrugged indifferently, but I was furious—I didn't care what she thought I'd do.

Susan gave me one last look, turned, and ran down the stairs toward the Magnas. It was only then that I saw Clouds standing by the forts, watching us intensely.

My heart was pounding. What was going on with Susan? And Clouds! I turned back into the school and was moping along the corridor when I heard a voice.

"Excuse me—it's Chris, isn't it?"

I turned. It was Mr. Evans, leaning out his class door.

"Didn't you read the special notices the other day?" he asked, smiling. "One of the new rules is absolutely no hanging out in the corridors."

"Oh . . . no, I didn't read them," I said, stepping back toward him and the school doors, my heart continuing to pound. I was about to walk by Mr. Evans and out of the school when I remembered the assembly resolution in my jacket pocket.

"Actually, Mr. Evans," I said, "I was kind of looking for *you*."

"For me?" he said, tilting his head.

"Yes," I said. "I have something to discuss with you."

"Discuss?" he said, smiling and turning back into his class. "Sounds very serious. We might need to sit down for this, don't you think?"

"Um, sure," I said, shrugging and stepping into his class. He pulled up a seat for me and sat at his desk.

"So, what is it you want to discuss?"

"Well," I said, reaching into my pocket. "It's something that a few students have written up. I was thinking you'd be the kind of teacher who would agree with what we, um, this group, like, thinks."

"Well, let's see what you've got then," he said, reaching across with a long arm and taking the folded page. I felt dizzy, like I was looking over the edge of a steep cliff—the point of no return.

While Mr. Evans read, I tried to keep myself calm by looking around his room. Mr. Evans was really into art so his walls were completely covered with paintings, sketches, and dangling paper shapes. I was studying an Egyptian mural at the back when he chuckled softly.

"Mr. Evans?" I asked.

"Oh, sorry, yes," he said, with a little smile, but then his face went serious. "A very interesting proposal. I think you should be able to run at least one assembly. I will sign the resolution, but I have just one question."

"Okay."

"Who is in this group of yours?"

I wasn't prepared for this question. I thought quickly. Who was the least suspicious member?

"Well," I said. "Susan Miranda . . . and a few others."

"Right," he said, grinning as he reached for a pen in

his shirt pocket and began to sign. "I don't suppose there are any troublemakers in this group?"

"Troublemakers? No, of course not. Just some students looking to, like, make some positive changes around here."

"Well," he said, finishing his signature with a swirl, "there you go, Chris. Good luck with your assembly and remember—if you ever need to talk, I'm here." He nodded at me, then pulled out some folders and started marking papers.

"Thanks, Mr. Evans," I said, stepping out of his classroom and into the corridor. I stopped outside, leaned against the wall, and closed my eyes.

One down, the rest of the teachers to go.

16

When I stepped into the apartment that afternoon, the phone was ringing. I wasn't grounded from the phone when my parents weren't home yet from work. I ran to grab the receiver. "Hello?"

"Bonjour, Monsieur Stren!" It was Clouds.

"Oh, hey," I said cautiously. We hadn't talked in ages, and I had no idea what he was up to.

"How goes the Revolution?" he asked.

"Well," I said, unable to hold back my pride. "I just got my first signature from Mr. Evans."

"Great!" he said. "And nice work by Boris, too."

"Yeah, amazing," I agreed. "I guess the haircut worked . . . and you're so good at pretending you know nothing at all."

"Thanks, man," he said. "It's hard. Inside I'm, like, throwing a party. So, I was wondering . . . do you wanna come down to my dad's place in the city on Saturday and stay overnight?"

"Really?"

"Yeah," he said. "I figure I owe you and . . . well . . . we can talk about our Acts of Dissent, and I just want to talk to you about something."

"Um, sure," I said, still cautious, but very curious. "But . . . I've got a problem."

"What?"

"My report card," I explained. "I tried to keep it away from Mom, but finally I had to show it, and now I'm grounded until further notice."

"Huh," he said. "Oh, well."

I suddenly wondered if the "something" Clouds wanted to talk about was Susan.

"But I can't let a stupid grounding get in my way," I declared.

"That's my man!" Clouds cheered.

"I'll figure something out, and call you later."

"When?"

"Sometime on Friday," I said. "I'm grounded from the phone at night, but Mom can't argue with me calling to say I can or can't come."

"Sounds like a plan," Clouds said.

"All right," I said. "Talk to you later."

That night, and for the next two days, I kept quiet at school. At home, I tried not to think about anything but school, and got right down to my homework. Mom was *really* checking my work every night. In class, after all of our brainstorming, we suddenly had a ton of individual assignments. Maybe this had been Mrs. Topper's plan all along. Anyway, I worked hard in class, staying there during break and lunch, and I went right home after school. I didn't want to see Susan, and it wasn't like I could talk to the other Revolutionists. I could tell Mom was impressed on Thursday, when I did homework all afternoon and evening. On Friday, after I did my math assignment, I found her in the kitchen making dinner.

"Mom? My French Revolution group for social studies is having another meeting tomorrow, and I was wondering if I could go."

She turned and looked at me. "Where and how long?"

"Um," I said, "that's the thing. Clouds has invited us all down to his dad's place in the city. His dad's sort of an expert on history."

"You mean like a professor?"

"Yeah," I lied. "I think so."

"I'd like to speak with him," she said, putting her finger to her mouth, thinking for a moment. "But how will you get there?"

"Bus. I've been saving up, from my work in the shop."

"Is that how everyone else is going?"

"Um . . . Yes," I said, laying down another lie.

"Hmmm," she said. "Well, I wanted to tell you—I talked to Mrs. Topper yesterday, and we're going to meet on Monday afternoon. She said she was glad I called. I guess she won't be so happy if I don't let you do your work." She paused. "You *have* been studying well the last couple of days, so okay, but I want to talk to Clouds's dad, and I'll need his number."

"Um, okay," I said. "Thanks."

I ran to the phone and dialed Clouds's number. He answered right away. "Clouds speaking."

"It's Chris."

"Hey," Clouds said. "What's up?"

"I can come," I said.

"Nice!" he said.

"The only thing is my mom wants to talk to your dad."

"We don't want that."

"No, we don't," I agreed.

"Ummm," he said, "when is she going to call?"

"Now?"

"Yeah, that's good. Perfect. Make sure she does call *right now*, okay?"

"I'll try," I said, wondering what he had up his sleeve. "I checked yesterday and there's a nine forty-five bus to the city, so I'll be arriving around eleven thirty. Can you pick me up?"

"Sure," he said. "Make sure she calls now. Talk to you later."

"Bye," I said.

Mom came into the kitchen. "Do you have the number?"

"Yep," I said. "Clouds said his dad's in now, so—"

"I should call," she interrupted, moving toward the phone. She punched in the number as I recited it. She mouthed "voicemail" to me. Clouds must have gotten on the phone so she couldn't get through. We were safe— temporarily.

I turned to hide that my heart was beating like crazy, and went to the living room and up my ladder. As I closed the hatch door, I heard my mother speak.

"Hello there," she said, to the voicemail. "This is Chris Stren's mother, Helen. I understand Chris is coming down to do some group work with Clouds in the city. I just wanted you to have our number in case there is a problem. So if you want to call I'm at . . ."

I stood up in the middle of the attic, put my hands together, and prayed that that was the only contact that Clouds's dad and my mom were going to have.

17

Clouds's dad didn't call back that night, and Mom was distracted when Dad came home with a furrowed brow and tales of his nightmare renovation. The next morning as I was leaving for the bus, Mom told me that she and Dad were going cross-country skiing for the day to give them both a well-deserved break. I was hoping that Clouds and I were completely off the hook.

The hour and a half bus ride to the city flew by. I brought the "L" encyclopedia volume to do some more detailed research on Lafayette, but my head was so jammed with thoughts, questions, and other concerns: What did Clouds want to talk to me about? What was his Dad like? Why did Susan dump me even though we weren't even really hanging out? What was Mom going to do to me when she found out I was lying about *everything*?

By the time I stepped off the bus, I was mentally wiped. Clouds wasn't, though. He grabbed the bag off my shoulder and gave me a welcoming slap on the back.

"This way, my man," he said. "I'm glad you were able to make it. We're gonna go to Beatnik Brews for some hot chocolate first, and then we'll go to my dad's."

Within minutes, we had made our way through busy city streets and arrived at the café.

"This is it!" he said. "Where ideas of revolution are born."

Clouds ordered us a couple of hot chocolates while I grabbed a table. He arrived with two steaming mugs and sat down.

"So," I said. "What did you want to tell me?"

"Oh," he said, looking down and taking a sip. He thought for a moment. "Well . . . there have been some new developments in Code: Topple the Tyrant."

"What's up?"

"Okay," he said, his eyes twinkling. "So the Penguin threw down the gauntlet with those new rules in the special school notices."

"Oh yeah," I said, not wanting to admit that my sheet was still stuffed in my desk in class.

"Yeah," he said, leaning forward, "I mean it was FULL of new rules. *No being in the corridors, no snowball fights, no snow forts.*" He leaned forward. "He might as well have declared war." Clouds looked out the window. "I'm going to seriously topple that tyrant."

"How?" I asked.

"Well, Lenon was big on speeches to the People. I figure I've got to rally the students during morning break or lunch. I just have to find the right moment."

"What are you going to say?"

"I'm not sure," he said. "I've got to defeat those new rules—all the rules—but I'm still in the planning stage."

He took a sip of hot chocolate.

"So," I said. "I got a signature from Mr. Evans, and I'm thinking Mrs. White will be my next victim. She was my sixth-grade teacher when my grades were better."

"Love it," he said, leaning in. "I was looking over the French Revolution stuff again yesterday. Pretty wild."

"Yeah." I agreed. "King Louis was powerful, but the people really showed him. They were starving and had had enough. He finally signed the petition, and then they had something called a constitutional monarchy which is sort of like what they have in Canada, I think. They didn't want to get rid of the king, they just wanted to take a lot of his power away."

"Oh yeah," Clouds said, shaking his head. "I was going to talk to you about that. I read about that Lafayette guy—he was a moderate, you know, which means he didn't go to extremes. Are you sure you want to follow in his steps? He kept on resigning, and he wasn't a real revolutionary. He was a stuffy aristocrat."

"I don't agree," I argued. "He was tough—he was the commander of the National Guard, which was like the army. He also fought in the American Revolution as a general. Anyway, Lafayette wanted things to be fair in France, so that people had more rights, but he didn't have to get rid of the king to do that."

"From what I read," Clouds countered, "the real revolutionists were the Jacobins. They wanted a republic for the people and they got right in there and demanded it."

"Don't worry," I said, feeling like he was trying to take over my Act of Dissent. "I know what I'm doing."

For a second, Clouds looked angry, but then he smiled.

"Fine," he said, shrugging.

"But," I said, trying to laugh it all off, "I just hope the Penguin doesn't give me trouble when I show him the resolution."

"The Penguin is no Louis the Sixteenth," Clouds stated. "Even though he thinks he is."

"I don't know how I'm going to do *anything* once Mom finds out about all the lies I'm telling."

"What do you mean?"

I told him the whole story, from the first lie about coming down to the city for a group meeting. Clouds was nodding with appreciation the whole way through.

"Well," he said, when I finished, "I've solved one of your problems."

"What do you mean?"

"Your mom called this morning,"

"She did? Did she talk to your Dad?"

"Nope, he was out," he said. "And . . . I filled in for him."

"You filled in for him?"

"Yeah," Clouds said, smiling mischievously. "Let's just say I can do a pretty good adult voice."

"Wow," I said, shaking my head. "And she believed you?"

"Yep—piece of cake."

"Well, thanks."

"No problem," he said, finishing off his mug. "There's an arcade around the corner that has Mission: Murder. Let's go play a few games . . . on me."

After playing video games for a couple of hours, we made our way to Clouds's dad's apartment. It was in an old brown-bricked row house. We went in the front door and climbed some stairs to a doorway. There was an envelope on the door. It said "Clouds" in black marker on the front.

"My Dad," Clouds said, smiling. He grabbed the envelope, inserted his key, and opened the door.

"Welcome to freedom and no rules!" Clouds exclaimed, as we entered the apartment. "Make yourself comfortable."

I flopped down on the couch, and Clouds went to the kitchen. I looked around: I'd never seen so many books in my life. There were rows of encyclopedias, stacks of old paperbacks, thin white journals, hardcover fiction books with bold lettering, and piles of reference books. He had a big old desk that Dad would have drooled over—if every inch of it hadn't been covered in more books. On one corner of the desk was a recent, close-up picture of Clouds.

"So," he said. "My dad drives a cab, and he's working

a twelve-hour shift. He was here for a sandwich and won't be back until four in the morning. He says there's a video card on top of the television and we can rent some movies on his account. So we've got the place to ourselves."

"Man, he works weird hours."

"Yeah, but he's own boss," Clouds said defensively.

"Sure, right," I said. "Hey, let's get some horror movies tonight!"

"Whatever you want," Clouds said, with a sparkle in his eye. "There's nothing stopping us."

It was one of the best nights I'd ever had. No parents and no reminders of my disastrous life back home. Clouds seemed different, too—I guess we both needed a break from revolution. We watched *Blood Flood I*, *II*, and *III* and wolfed down several bowls full of popcorn. During the last movie, late in the night, I was feeling a bit sick from of all the butter and guts. I closed my eyes on the couch for a moment to settle my stomach, and it was the last thing I remembered.

Clouds woke me up the next morning.

"Mr. Sleepy Head," he whispered. "Your bus is leaving soon."

"What time is it?" I questioned with a yawn.

"Shhh," Clouds said, pointing down a hallway. "My dad is asleep in his room."

"I'm sorry," I whispered, rubbing my eyes. "I guess every household has its rules."

"It's not a rule," Clouds snapped. "It's just . . . common courtesy."

I was too tired to argue. "What time is it?" I asked.

"It's ten past ten."

"What?!" I whispered, bolting up and scrambling around. "My bus is leaving in twenty minutes. I can't be late, or I'm dead."

"I know," Clouds whispered back. "Don't worry, though. We went in a bit of circle yesterday. It's just a ten-minute walk."

I grabbed my things, and started stuffing them into my bag.

"Oh, hey," he said. "I have that winter hat I borrowed from you when I stayed over. It's in my room."

"Okay," I said impatiently as he turned away.

As I waited by the door, I looked around. In front of me, on a table was a picture of Clouds and what looked like his mom and dad.

"Here it is," he whispered as he approached. He stood in front of the picture. "By the way, Chris, you didn't tell anyone, like Susan, about my mom and the, um, conversation I had with her on the phone, did you?"

"No," I said. "Of course not."

"Good, because that *never* happens," he said. "I have my mom wrapped around my finger." He paused. "But you don't have to keep *this* visit a secret from the Revolutionists. Everyone should know about my rule-less life with my dad."

"Um, sure, whatever," I said. "By the way, what were you going to tell me that was so important?"

"I told you already at Beatnik Brews," he said, "about the progress of Code: Topple the Tyrant."

"It wasn't about Susan?"

"No," Clouds said, "why?"

"Oh, nothing," I said. "It's a long story. I'll tell you later."

"Okay," he said, opening the door. "Thanks for coming, man. This was great."

"Yeah, it was," I said and ran out the door and down the stairs to the street.

On the bus, I pulled out the encyclopedia volume and reread about Lafayette.

On July 14, 1789, three days after Lafayette presented the original draft of his resolution, French peasants stormed a prison called the Bastille, and freed some political prisoners that King Louis had imprisoned. A month and a half later, a final draft of the Declaration of the Rights of Man and of the Citizen was adopted, and some real changes began. . . .

I was sleepy from the motion of the bus and was about to close the volume when something caught my eye. It said that in October of that year, Lafayette actually saved King Louis and Queen Marie Antoinette from a furious crowd outside the palace. So he wasn't a revolutionist—he *was* actually in support of the king.

I closed my eyes. Maybe Clouds was right. If Lafayette wasn't a real revolutionist, maybe I shouldn't follow his life. After all, I wasn't like Lafayette at all. I certainly wasn't a commander of any army and I definitely wasn't in the position to save any queen.

PART 4

Who's the Tyrant Now?

18

I would have been bored stiff at assembly on Monday if I hadn't been so worried about my mom's meeting with Mrs. Topper for later that afternoon—my heart was pounding like crazy. And then when the Penguin was finishing his assembly address, he actually grabbed my attention for once.

"I'm sure by now, students," he said, "that you have read the school notices and the new rules."

Clouds sat up in the row ahead of me.

"Regardless," the Penguin continued, "I think it's important to review them with you now." He paused. "First, there will be absolutely no snow forts on school grounds, before, during, or after school hours. They are very dangerous and hide students from view of the teacher on duty."

Clouds threw his hands up and shook his head like this was outrageous. I wasn't so sure—the Penguin sort of had a point.

"Second," Principal Dorfman continued, "we've had a lot of unattended hallway roamers at break and lunch time these days. There will be *no one* in the hallways at these times. Teachers have been told to remind students to use the washroom on the way out to the schoolyard."

There were a few groans. "And—quiet please—and complaints of the cold are not legitimate, and will not exempt students from being outside. If students wear winter coats, mittens, and hats, you should be just fine."

Clouds mouthed "*What?*" looking around him at other students.

Mrs. Topper leaned forward and whispered, "Clouds . . . that's enough."

"Third," the Penguin continued, as his eyes locked on Clouds, "a student recently alerted me to the fact that 'No Throwing Snowballs' is not in the rulebook. This was an oversight on my part, or perhaps I assumed this was obvious. In any case, there will be *absolutely* no snowballs thrown on school grounds, before, during, and after school."

Clouds continued to scan the room for revolt, but there was silence in the auditorium.

"Now," the Penguin concluded, "we'll move on to the teacher announcements . . ."

I watched as Clouds's shoulders sank, and he didn't budge for the rest of assembly.

On my way back to class, I stopped for a book at my locker, where a note fell to my feet. It said:

Meet in Sterling Woods. Same spot. 3:45 p.m. Make sure no one sees you.

I barely had time to consider the new Revolutionist meeting, because as soon as I got to class we were on our way to the library to do more work on our research projects. I worked hard all day, hoping that Mrs. Topper would notice, and be more sympathetic when speaking to Mom.

After the final bell, I made my way to our meeting spot in Sterling Woods. Everyone was early, and I was the last to approach from the road. I took them all in from a distance: Boris's closely cropped black hair was growing longer. Susan looked really stressed; she had these worried wrinkles on her forehead. She glanced at me, but I looked away. Landry paced back and forth between trees, like usual, and Clouds looked impatient to get the meeting going.

"Hey, Chris," he said. "Time to get started. What a week we had! First of all, I'd like to congratulate Boris on his successful revolt against boring education."

Boris grinned. "Yeah, thanks. Everything is going as planned. The boring lessons have stopped." He spoke with tranquility. "I have also started a morning meditation meeting on Mondays and Fridays. I am trying to start a group called 'Bullies Against Bullying,' but I'm having trouble getting Terrence on my side. Once he joins, all the tough guys far and wide will come begging for a slice of my peaceful pie."

Landry couldn't stop himself from laughing. "Hey, Mr. Great Soul! If your revolt is such a success, then why are we doing so much work and researching our brains off?"

"Research is an important part of learning, Landry. If you weren't running through the bookshelves like a slalom skier all class, maybe you would know that."

"Yeah, well, we'll see," Landry maintained, tossing a paper airplane, made from an old crumpled-up detention slip.

"Jeez! Litterbug," Boris said, picking up the airplane and stuffing it in his pocket.

"Okay, okay," Clouds chimed in. "Even though there was some progress last week, the rest of us still have a lot of work to do. Let's have an update from each of the rest of the Revolutionists. Then, we'll make more plans. Chris, what's up with you?"

I pulled out the Assembly Resolution and waved it in front of me. "I've got one signature so far, from Mr. Evans. My next prospect is Mrs. White, because she's always been nice to me. But not every teacher will be as easy. So last night I was thinking that each of you could get this thing signed by the teachers you know best. Except maybe Clouds, since he's only been around for a couple of weeks."

"Mr. Singh is the track coach," Landry jumped in. "He thinks I'm smooth. Yep, that's right! Smooooooooth. Like butter on bread. Like cheese spread on crackers."

"Mr. Danforth runs chess club," Boris offered. "He'll be like putty in my hands."

"Yeah," Susan said, not quite looking me in the eye. "I'm pretty sure I can show it to a few teachers. The only one I'll have trouble with is Mrs. Crespin. For some reason, she always picks on girls. Clouds could probably get a signature from her."

"I look forward to it," Clouds said, smiling and rubbing his hands together. "So we'll go through—"

"Um," I interrupted, looking at my watch. "Sorry, Clouds, I'm on a seriously tight schedule. Things have been totally crazy at home for me these days. Actually, my mom and Mrs. Topper are meeting right now about my report card."

"Oh, jeez," Landry said. "I know how that goes."

"Yeah," I said. "My grades were pretty bad, but when she finds out this group isn't a school group, well . . . I'm dead."

"Oh, gosh," Susan said, looking guilty.

"Yeah," I said, avoiding Susan's gaze and looking at Clouds, his arms crossed. "So, everyone, um, don't count on talking to me on the phone in the near future, and we'll see how dead I am in an hour or so."

"Can you stay or should we go ahead without you?" Clouds challenged, winking at Susan.

"Um, I'll stay," I said, feeling a rush of jealousy. "Definitely for a bit."

"Okay, Suz, what's up?" Clouds demanded.

"Well," Susan said, "it's still January, so even though the Magnas aren't aware of it, Sherry is still the official leader. Even Sherry doesn't realize it yet, actually. Anyway, she and I have been hanging out more at break and lunch, and I think she's beginning to see things my way. The Three Cs are my next direct targets. If I can get one of them on my side, I can get them all. Meanwhile, Harriet and Alita are, like, enemies Number One and Two. I have to get them away from the Cs for long enough so I can use my powers of persuasion. This is how the queen would have done it. And I need to get my hands on that Magna Charter—I just know it's going to help me somehow."

Boris jumped in. "I think I've heard about that Magna thing before from somewhere else."

"We can't account for what happens in that shaved cranium of yours," Susan said, grinning. "Maybe the meditation is getting you mixed up."

Boris scratched his head in thought.

"Anyway," Susan continued, "I was telling you about Queen Elizabeth. The first thing she did was have great advisors. Her chief advisor, William Cecil, got her through a lot of jams with her enemies in and out of the country. Because of the way Clouds handled the Magnas so well on his first day at school, I have chosen him as my top advisor."

I eyed Clouds, who looked like he already knew this was coming.

"As for the rest of you," she continued, "I have a pretty tall order to ask. There's going to be some weird stuff happening with me and the Magnas in the next little while, and I'm not exactly sure how it's going to go. There's a chance that I will have to sort of call on each of you to get mixed up in the chaos. If I haven't spoken to you about anything beforehand, just play along with whatever seems right. I'll try not to put you into a situation you can't handle."

"You mean, Sherry could come up to me and say, 'Go over to Alita and pull her hair,' and then I'm supposed to do it?" Landry asked, with a hint of pleasure curling over his lips.

"Exactly. Don't think about it—just do it." Susan was so worked up that she missed Landry's joke.

"But, hopefully," Clouds added, "we'll be able to warn you about it." It sounded as if Clouds and Susan had already talked about this at length. "Now, as for Code: Topple the Tyrant, sometime this month I'm going to begin to make speeches during lunch and break. Lenon was a great speechmaker. His first step was rallying all the people to his side."

"What was his side?" Boris probed.

"Well, czars, who were Russian kings, had been running Russia for hundreds of years and it wasn't that they were all totally evil or anything, it was just that there were a lot of peasants with no money, no food, and no control over their lives—like in France, in the French Revolution. So Lenon came in and wanted to overthrow the Czar and give the power to the people."

"And, what's *your* side?" Boris pressed.

"Well, I just want to take the Penguin down."

"Could you be more specific?" Boris said.

"No," Clouds snapped.

"Didn't you say something to me the other day about going after the new rules?" I asked.

"Maybe," Clouds said, not looking at me. "I can't share everything—a leader just needs to take total control at a certain point. You just need to know this, Revolutionists: when I start making my speeches, all of you should wait until other students come to listen before you jump in, like we did for Boris's Act."

Boris nodded but looked like he wasn't satisfied by Clouds's response.

"Sorry to interrupt again, but I gotta go," I said, turning. "I have to get home before my mom—I need every advantage I can get."

Clouds sighed audibly. "Fine . . . Wait! Listen up, everyone. Let's say, from now on, you'll know a meeting's been called when you hear one of us say 'Revolution.'"

"So how'd the group project go on Saturday?" my mother said, standing over me an hour later.

She had just arrived home and found me studying at the living room table.

"Ummm," I said, trying to gauge if she was setting a trap. "Fine?"

"Did you get a lot of work done?"

"Yep."

"On what?" my mother demanded, crossing her arms.

"Well, I've been studying the French Revolution, so I told the group about how the Estates General—the kind of, like, parliament—was called to meet for the first time in over a hundred fifty years. The people were starving and had no way of changing their position in life, so they wanted to have something called 'civil equality.' King Louis kept on trying to get rid of them, but they wouldn't go away. Finally they got him to sign the Declaration of the Rights of Man and of the Citizen . . . um . . . do you want to hear more?"

My mother looked at me like I was an alien.

"Chris, what the heck is going on?" she snapped. "You come home with a terrible report card, Mrs. Topper isn't happy with your work, and you have been working in a study group that *doesn't exist*!"

I closed my books and ran my hands through my hair.

"Let me explain," I said.

"Yes," she said. "NOW."

"Well, when Clouds came to us, me and the, um, other group members, he said he wanted to kind of study different stuff from what we were doing in class."

"What did Mrs. Topper think about this?" she asked.

"She doesn't know about it, actually," I said.

"That's funny," she said. "Because when I mentioned your work on the French Revolution with this group, her eyes lit up. She said, 'Let me guess who is in this posse.' And she proceeded to name Landry and Boris."

"What about Susan and Clouds?" I demanded.

"Hey, *I'm* the one asking questions here. So . . . how does she know it was those guys in your group?"

"I don't know," I said. "A wild guess?"

"That's what she said. Something funny is going on. I can just feel it."

"Look," I said, going for broke. "Okay, so I should have been doing my real schoolwork, but you aren't going to punish me for trying to learn something new, are you? And I've been working really hard these days, and—"

"Okay, Crick, okay," she said, pausing to think for a moment. "Just . . . just tell me nothing funny is going on."

I looked at her and thought about it.

"Okay," I said. "Nothing funny is going on." This was actually true—whatever was going on wasn't funny at all. "So, am I still grounded?"

Just then the phone rang, and Mom got up to get it.

"I guess not," she said, "but you are on serious probation." She picked up the phone. "Hello?"

There was a silence and then Mom said, "Okay, one second," and put her hand over the receiver. "Crick, time to study. Upstairs in your room. Now."

I wondered who it was on the phone, but it wasn't like I was going to risk picking up my line to find out. Besides, the person on the other end of the phone was the least of my worries.

19

Mrs. White took school grounds duty very, very seriously. That's why when I found her by the field at break the next day, it was hard to get her undivided attention.

"Um, Mrs. White," I said, "I was wondering if you would read this resolution some of us have drawn up."

She nodded, not taking her eyes off the field, and grabbed the sheet. "What is it?"

"Well," I said, trying to get into her line of vision. "Some of us think the assembly should be more student-focused and we are looking for some teacher support."

"Mark Mowers!" she yelled across the field. "No wrestling, please."

She looked down at the resolution and began to read when a younger student ran up in a panic.

"Something bad is happening at the new fort," he announced.

"What new fort?" she asked, dropping the resolution to her side. "There shouldn't be a new fort."

"Yeah, well," he said, "Terrence and a bunch of guys have trapped some seventh graders in a new snow fort hidden behind the gully, and they are saying that they are going to collapse it on top of them. Boris was trying to stick up for them so he, like, threw himself in front of them, and then Terrence and his friends grabbed Boris and put him in the garbage can and—"

Mrs. White marched off toward the hubbub, not realizing she still had the resolution in her hand.

"Um, Mrs. White," I said, trailing after her. "The resolution. Could you sign it?"

"Oh yes, right," she said, scribbling her name at the bottom. "Interesting idea, Chris. Good luck."

As she hurried off, I looked down at my resolution. There were no fireworks and no balloons, but I had landed my *second* signature!

My success was short-lived. In minutes, I saw a troop of Magnas heading toward me. Harriet and Alita were in the lead, flanked by Zigi and Emma from my class. I looked desperately around for Susan on the school grounds, but she was nowhere to be seen. My eyes fell on Clouds about a hundred feet away. He nodded at me.

Harriet arrived first, leaning toward me, her breath a sickly sweet mint. "Which guy is Susan going to the Ten Mile Skate with?"

The Ten Mile Skate? I'd completely forgotten that it was this coming weekend. The Ten Mile Skate was a winter tradition, in which much of the town skated along the Laverton River to the old dam and back. When I was younger I used to race with my friends, but last year, some of my classmates actually took dates. Doug and I just went with a bunch of other guys, and we played tag and threw snowballs at each other.

"Um . . . I . . . I have no idea," I replied.

"Come on, you can tell us!" Harriet said.

"We won't tell anyone!" Alita added.

"Who, Chris?" Emma said. "Tell us now."

I looked around trying to find some guidance, but now none of the Revolutionists were in sight. Susan certainly wasn't doing the Ten Mile Skate with *me*.

"If you had to guess," Harriet demanded. "Who would it be? Come on! You know who she's been hanging out with recently, don't you?"

I thought of Clouds and got a lump in my throat.

"I have *no* idea," I snapped. "Go away."

"Don't give us that!" said Alita. "You know exactly who it is. You're just sad about it. Boohoo for Chris."

I wanted to argue, but I knew better. I turned my back on them and began to walk away. They followed behind, still questioning me, so that it looked like I was leading a small parade across the field. I spotted Mrs. White, now on snow fort patrol, and approached her desperately.

"Hello, Mrs. White!" I said, too sweetly. "Thanks for your help today."

The Magnas faded away like vampires from garlic.

"Why, I'm always happy to lend a hand," she said, smiling, but looking toward the school. I followed her gaze. Boris was nowhere in sight, but the Penguin had a hand on Clouds's shoulder and was leading him into the school.

Then Susan exited the school doors and didn't even look at Clouds. She was preparing for another encounter: the Magnas were speeding toward her like storm.

Out of the corner of my eye, I saw Landry heading my way. I was glad; I had something to tell him. He ran indirectly toward me in a long, arching curve. I looked back at Mrs. White, who had moved closer to the forts. When we were within a couple of feet of each other, I whispered, "Revolution," and it took me two seconds to realize that he had whispered the exact same thing.

Just my luck, I came face-to-face with Harriet and Alita on the way to Sterling Woods after school. They eyed me suspiciously as I walked by, with no reply to my meek hello. A horror movie tingle went down my spine. I waited at the Happy Holiday Motel sign until I was sure they weren't watching and raced into the woods. I was the first to arrive at our meeting spot, but within five minutes, I heard someone huffing and puffing through the trees.

"Susan . . . Clouds," Boris gasped as he arrived, ". . . caught . . . Harriet . . . Alita . . . *trouble!*"

He braced himself against a tree and tried to catch his breath.

"What do you mean? Were Susan and Clouds walking together?" I said, trying not to sound as jealous as I was feeling.

"I dunno," he said. "Maybe they stopped worrying about

being seen together. I was walking along Sunnydale when I came up to the four of them. I made like I had no idea what was going on. Everyone thinks I'm crazy now anyway, so I just gave a little prayer bow and kept walking."

"Did you hear anything they were saying?" I asked.

"Nothing. I just—"

Landry came running through the woods. We watched as he ran through birch trees like it was an obstacle course. He stopped a few paces from us and stared.

"What's with the faces? Who died?"

"No one died," I said, "but Magnas caught Clouds and Susan on Sunnydale. Didn't you see?"

"No, I came through the woods," Landry said.

"Well . . . it didn't look good," Boris stated, as if Landry was to blame.

"Not to worry, folks," Landry said, swaggering around us, with his thumbs in his coat pockets like a bow-legged cowboy. "It's Clouds. He'll take care of everything. He always does."

I leaned against the tree the way Clouds always did.

"Okay," I said, taking charge. "Landry's right. We can't worry about what's happening to Clouds and Susan. There's nothing we can do about it. Let's talk about what happened over the last twenty-four hours."

"Well," Landry said, "Hairier and Airheada came up to me and asked who Susan was going to the Ten Mile Skate with."

"I got the same at break," I said, smirking at Landry's nicknames.

"I told them at lunch," Boris said, pushing his glasses up his nose, "that if they'd just follow the virtues of Satyagraha, things like who is going to the Ten Mile Skate with who would become immaterial."

Landry pointed a finger at Boris, like a teacher. "Did you tell them that they'd have to shave their craniums and learn how to put both feet behind their heads?"

"No," Boris said, closing his eyes and looking like he was trying to meditate Landry out of existence. He opened his eyes and turned to me. "When I started talking to Harriet and Alita about Truth, Determination, and Nonviolence they seemed to lose interest."

"Yeah, I can relate," Landry said. "Well, who *is* Susan going with? What about you, Chris? How'd your date go?"

"Fine," I said. "And none of your business."

"What'd you do? Did you kiss? Did you, like—"

"Landry," I snapped. "I *don't* want to talk about it."

"Fine," he said, pretending to be hurt. "Be that way."

"You know . . . I bet . . ." Boris exclaimed. "I bet Susan was trying to distract those girls long enough to get the Three Cs on her side."

"Well, she could have given us some warning," Landry said, wincing. "Just the smell of those girls, close up and breathing all over you, is like one big, stinky, gross, disgusting—"

"Wait!" Boris whispered, lurching at Landry and covering his mouth. "Listen!"

Landry pushed Boris away, but kept quiet. We heard voices and soon enough, Clouds's and Susan's rosy faces emerged from the trees.

"What the heck is going on here?" Clouds said, glaring at me. "You running a meeting without us?"

I stood up straight. "Um, no, I just—"

"We were just trying to figure out what the heck was going on," Boris said, unable to contain himself. "When I saw you and Susan, I just freaked out! What were they saying to you? Why were you together? Weren't we supposed to walk alone?"

"Whoa, Boris," Susan said. "Want to take a moment to meditate?"

Boris shrugged as Clouds made his way toward the tree. There was an awkward moment, and then I relinquished his spot.

"Okay, that's better," he announced, clearing his throat. "Susan has been busy today. Chris's chat with Harriet and company gave Susan enough time to talk with the Cs. Good work."

"Yeah," Susan said, "they were into it . . . I think. They said they had felt really weird about Harriet and Alita taking over in the fall, but didn't know what to do about it. But let's backtrack a bit. Last night I called Harriet about the Magna Charter, and she said it was none of my business. So I figured I'd follow in Queen Elizabeth's footsteps and bluff. I told Harriet that I'd talked to Tina Nelson, a Magna from last year, and she said that all Magnas had a right to see the charter."

"Why didn't you *really* talk to Tina?" Boris asked. "Couldn't you just tell on Harriet and Alita to get the Magnas back on track that way?"

"No chance," Susan said, shaking her head. "Some of this disaster is my and the rest of the Magnas' fault. We've been total pushovers, and haven't stuck up for the tradition of the Magnas. I don't want *any* former Magnas to know how badly we've failed."

"So what *did* Harriet say?" Landry demanded.

"She said, 'Fine, I'll bring it tomorrow,' and then I couldn't sleep a wink last night thinking she was going to call Tina to find out that I was lying and—"

"This is killing me," Landry said, putting his hands to his forehead. "Just spit it out! Did you get the Magna Chart-thingy?"

"Yes," Susan said. "Harriet secretly handed it over this morning, and she seemed really worried. She said I could only have it until tomorrow so before I show it to the other Magnas I really wanted to show you guys what was in it, so I called—"

"So *I* called a meeting," Clouds interrupted.

"Um, right," Susan said, looking at Clouds confused, "but there's more, guys. It seems as if Harriet and Alita did some homework because they came looking for me on Sunnydale, and they said they talked to Tina and she had no idea what they were talking about and then they demanded to have the charter back."

"But Boris said that Clouds was with you too!" Landry blurted out.

I kept silent.

"Sheesh, I'm getting to that," she said, glaring at Landry. "I didn't know what to do. . . . I was saying how the Magna Charter was at home, when Clouds suddenly showed up and started talking." She looked over at him. "He said he wanted to discuss the student council and the new school rules, and then Boris passed by and did that weird Gandhi bow without saying a word, which pretty much freaked everyone out, and then I started blabbing on about student council protocol, and Harriet and Alita suddenly got really antsy. Then Harriet made up some story about her piano lesson, and they took off."

"What *were* you doing there, Clouds?" I asked.

"Well," he said, "whenever I walk to a meeting I go along the woods, but close to the street, so that I can keep an eye on things. I *always* like to keep an eye on things. You can't be too careful." He looked at all of us strangely and suspiciously. "Anyway, today I saw Susan leaving the school gates so I just tailed beside her in the woods. When I saw Harriet and Alita approaching her, I knew it couldn't be a coincidence. So I jumped out to help."

Susan nodded. "And lucky that he did, because I was able to keep *this*." She pulled out an old, yellowed notebook. "It looks like it's an old spelling book from way back. But inside is a whole list of official rules for the Magnas, including some that I've never heard about. I'm not supposed to share any of this with you—it's top secret." She passed it to Boris. "But you can take a look while I explain what I found. Most of it is just wacko 1950s stuff, but on page eleven, under Leadership of the Magnas: Rule twenty-seven, it says that if any monthly leader wants to make changes to the Magnas rules, they can do so as long as they have fifty percent support. A vote can be called by the leader, which can be taken at any time. So all Sherry and I have to do is—"

Boris giggled. "Check this out. 'Magnas members must always wear their hair in ponytails, their skirts ironed and their socks pulled up high.'"

"Susan," he said, eyeing her up and down, "I'm afraid you have not complied with Magnas rules. The jeans, the loose hair! They just won't do."

"Funny, Boris," Susan smirked. "I told you some of it is a little out there, but the stuff the Magnas were taught last spring is also—"

"Wait!" Boris said, throwing up a finger. "I knew I knew something about this!"

"Wait!" Landry said. "I knew he knew he knew something about this!"

"Will someone not dedicated to peace please shut him up?" Boris exclaimed.

"Landry," Clouds said, glaring at him.

"Thank you," Boris said. "Okay, it says right here at the

beginning: 'The Magna Charter is based on the historical event of the signing of the Magna *Carta*.' That's it! I
was watching a history show on TV the other day, and I
learned the Magna Carta was this document that all these
English nobles drew up, and they got the too-powerful
king, I think it was King John, to sign it around eight
hundred years ago. The Magna Carta made it so that the
king had way less power."

"Yeah, I was going to mention all that," Susan said,
nodding. "And there's more background: way back in
1956, the year before *this* Magna Charter was written,
there were some eighth-grade girls at Laverton Middle
School who started a secret group. Early on, one of the
members became a tyrant just like Harriet, and all the
others finally called a meeting to stop it. One of the girls
was a British history buff or something because they decided to base their revolt and resolution on something
that happened in the 1200s in Britain. Look at the back,
Boris: You can see all the original girls signed it, and then
they became the Magnas. Pearl Dobson, at the bottom,
was the tyrant."

We all leaned over to look.

"Hold on," Boris said, pulling the book away and flip-
ping to the front again. "There's nothing about those 1956
details in here, and this is dated June 5, 1957."

"Yeah," Susan said, "I had to do some top-secret historical research."

"Okay, okay," Clouds said, seeming impatient. "So

Susan and Sherry will propose a rule change. They are going to call a meeting tomorrow because next Wednesday it's February and the reins are handed over to Harriet. If Sherry and Susan have the support of the Three Cs, then that's five out of ten, and they'll have fifty percent of the vote. Done! They can agree to return to their old ways of secrecy, equality, respect." He paused. "So, after what happened today with the Penguin, I'm ready to get started on Code: Topple the Tyrant very soon."

"Wait," Landry said. "What did happen after the Penguin found our secret fort?"

"Well," Clouds said. "The Penguin dragged me to the office, sat me down, and had me read from the rule handbook—the suspension section! It said, 'Students found breaking a school rule will receive one warning, and then if that student repeats the rule infraction, he or she can be suspended.'"

"So, you'd better stop building forts then," Susan said.

"No way," Clouds stated.

"But—"

"Chris," he interrupted, "We need to get this meeting moving. How goes the Assembly Resolution?"

"Okay," I said, shrugging at Susan, who was obviously upset and staring at Clouds. "I've got signatures from Mr. Evans and Mrs. White. I'm going to pass the resolution off to you guys, now," I said, handing it to Boris. "You get Mr. Danforth's signature, then pass the resolution on to Landry for Mr. Singh. Clouds, you are on for Mrs. Crespin, and then Susan, you'll get Mr. McNally and Mrs. Deercroft and anyone else if you can."

"I'll do my best," she said, shrugging, "but I make no promises. Things have been pretty crazy in Susan Miranda's life."

She smiled weakly at me. It was better than nothing.

"I'm concerned about something here," said Landry, who had grabbed the Magna Charter from Boris. "There's one important rule that must stay on here if I am to agree with Susan's changes."

"What's that, Lan?" Susan inquired earnestly.

"'No Listening to Elvis Presley *At Any Time*,'" Landry spluttered, howling as he said it. "Down with the King, dudes! Down with the King."

We all laughed.

"Hey," I said. "Before I forget. The reason why I called a meeting—"

"You called the meeting?" Clouds snapped. "*I* called the meeting. You're trying to take over, aren't you?" He didn't sound like he was joking.

"No," I said, flabbergasted. "I just wanted to tell you guys that I sort of escaped trouble with my mom, but *we* . . . um . . . didn't. I was ungrounded because, well, I lied again. I said we just wanted to learn better stuff than in class. But Mom told Mrs. Topper about us and without any help, Mrs. Topper named Boris and Landry as members of our group."

"Oh no," Landry said.

"For once, Landry, I agree with you," Boris said, shaking his head. "I don't know how long I can keep this up."

"Chris, your mom didn't say anything to her about me, did she?" Susan said, wincing.

"I don't think so, but I wasn't exactly in the position to interrogate her."

"It's okay," Clouds said, turning and almost standing right in front of me. "We all screw up sometimes, Chris. But make sure it doesn't happen again."

"I didn't screw up, Clouds," I insisted, standing my ground and looking him in the eye.

He stared at me for a moment, looked at the others, and then said, "So, now we have to be *really* careful at school, and from now on, only *I* call meetings . . . and end them. Meeting adjourned."

"Fine," I said, turning. "I've got a ton of homework tonight, anyway, and until my next report card, I'm going to have no life."

"So, who are you going to the Ten Mile Skate with this year?" Mom asked at the dinner table that night. Dad was still working on a big renovation job out of town.

"Why?" I snapped, making a mountain of my potatoes and excavating a hole to make a lake.

"I'm just curious, Chris."

I shrugged. "It's just stupid kids' stuff," I said. "And anyway, I've got too much homework to do."

"But you've always loved the Ten Mile Skate," she said,

ladling some gravy for herself and passing it over. "Well, what about your friend, Clouds? Isn't he going?"

"Clouds?" I said, shrugging. "I don't know."

"Hmmm. There *is* something strange about that boy. I don't know what it is. Are you sure you should be hanging out with him?"

"This is *just great*, Mom!" I said, my temper rising suddenly. "First you make sure Doug isn't in my class or *my friend* and now you're trying to do the same with Clouds."

"Okay, Crick, okay," she said. "You just seem a little . . . distant these days. I didn't realize you felt so strongly. What's happening with your other friend, Susan? How's she doing—"

"Mom!" I snapped, slamming my fork down on my plate. "I DON'T KNOW. Why won't people stop asking me about Susan?! Can I be excused, please?"

She looked at me sternly for a moment, and then her eyes softened. "Okay, Chris."

I cleared my dishes, went up the ladder, and flopped onto my couch. I didn't feel like doing any homework. I didn't feel like doing anything. I felt sad about Susan, but that wasn't it. Clouds was changing, everything was changing, and I didn't like it one bit.

20

Landry was running around the school grounds the next day at break, whispering something to everyone as he passed. He finally got near enough to me, and I heard him say, "Power to the students! Come to the basketball court to find out how to start a revolution! Power to the students!"

A small crowd was already gathering at the court. I hurried over, and shouldered into the crowd. Clouds was standing on a milk crate in front of about thirty students. I saw Boris with a few of his seventh-grade disciples, but couldn't see Susan, or any of the Magnas for that matter. I looked around for the teacher on duty, and couldn't find one. Then I focused on Clouds's words.

". . . And so I ask you. What's the deal with the new rules? No one in the school hallways during break? What if there's an emergency? Anyone ever hear of a bathroom break? Why are the teachers allowed in the hallways then?" I saw a couple of students nodding, others tilting their heads suspiciously. "And then there's the one about no snow forts? What does the Penguin think—we're idiots? How are we supposed to have any creative fun around here? We aren't allowed to play hockey at break, and snow soccer is way more dangerous than building snow forts. So, people of Laverton Middle School, I, Clouds McFadden, propose to do something about it!" He raised his fist in the air. "Power to the Students!" There was an enthusiastic murmur. "We're being pushed around. What do we hear *all the time*? 'Be quiet! Do as you're told! Sit down! Do your homework. No this. No that.'" A few supportive 'yeahs' were shouted out from the crowd. "And now there's even *more* rules? Come on! It's time to fight back and—"

Landry suddenly jumped onto the crate. He whispered something in Clouds's ear and pointed toward the school doors. I got on my tiptoes to look, and saw Mrs. Deercroft speeding our way. I looked at Clouds, who seemed unfazed.

"Remember, everyone," he said, in a slightly softer voice. "Power to the students!" He paused for a moment then said, "Also, remember: not a word about what I said. Now get lost, or we'll get in *big* trouble." And at that, he threw his hands out at the crowd, shooing us like alley cats.

It was amazing. Everyone followed his orders and scattered. As for Clouds, I watched as Landry ushered him away toward the gully. Within seconds, Mrs. Deercroft was at the abandoned milk crate, looking around suspiciously, but Clouds was out of sight.

When I entered the classroom several minutes later, Landry and Clouds were already in their seats, rosy-cheeked and ready for work. I could not catch their attention, nor could I figure out how they'd gotten to class so quickly. Then I remembered: Clouds had said something about building a secret snow tunnel. I looked at Boris, who shrugged his shoulders and widened his eyes. The rest of the students gathered around Clouds, but he wouldn't speak, and waved them away. Mrs. Topper came in and sent everyone to their seats. After quieting us down, she announced the due dates for our assignments, which took the wind out of everyone's revolutionary sails.

At lunch, a note dropped out of my locker. I checked up and down the hall, and picked it up. It said:

> *Call me at 4 p.m. today.*
> *SM*

I strolled down the corridor, wondering what Susan wanted to talk about. I was expecting to see Clouds making another speech at the basketball courts, but instead, I saw him and Landry hurrying back toward the gully, followed by a few new Revolutionists who had listened to his speech. Boris was on the opposite side of the field trying to break up a fight between two sixth graders. Then I noticed something different going on with the Magnas— Susan, the Three Cs, Sherry and Maria were hanging out by the baseball diamond backstop while Harriet, Alita, Zigi, and Emma remained at the basketball courts. Both groups were in heated discussions, occasionally throwing nasty glances toward each other. It looked like Susan had made her big move.

I was alone again when I got home from school. Mom was at the hospital and Dad was still working on the out-of-town renovation. I couldn't concentrate on homework, so I paced the kitchen.

When the clock finally ticked to four o'clock, I grabbed the phone and dialed Susan's number.

"Hello?"

"Um, hi. It's Chris."

"Great," Susan said. "I'm so glad you called. I haven't been able to talk to *anyone*."

"Really?" I said, sarcastically. "What about Clouds?"

"What do you mean? I haven't talked to him in days."

"Oh," I said, surprised.

"Well," she said, "except for at the meeting and before with Harriet and Alita. But he was acting crazy. Everyone is acting crazy these days—I don't even know where to start."

"How about with the Magnas?" I said, for once glad instead of nervous to be talking to her. "That looked serious."

"You're not kidding," she said, sighing. "I finally talked to Sherry about the Monthly Leadership and showed her the Magna Charter. She's totally in! She called a meeting at break yesterday at the back of the school—that's why we weren't at the basketball court during Clouds's speech.

Anyway, I read out Rule Twenty-seven about how the official leader, Sherry, had a right to make a vote for change, and the change she wanted was to become *real* Magnas again: secret, equal, and respectful. Harriet was totally fuming. She said, 'That old Magna stuff is so yesterday. What's the point if everything is secret and you don't have any power?' and I tried to argue, but Alita jumped in and said, 'Whatever. This is a total waste of time.'"

"Then what did you do?" I asked.

"I said, 'Let's put it to a vote,' and Harriet looked around at everyone and said, 'Okay, fine, Ms. Student Council Suck-up.'"

"Whoa. Then what happened?"

"Well, I was really nervous I was going to lose everyone," Susan said, gulping. "Harriet is so intimidating . . . but in the end it was five versus five, enough to pass a rule. But then Emma said, 'This book is stupid,' and she tried to grab it out of my hands and I tugged back and the Magna Charter ripped." She paused and sighed. "So Harriet said, 'There. Now the rules are destroyed, and we can forget about what the Magnas *used* to be. Who's with me?' Alita, Zigi, Emma, and Maria went right to her side, and the Three Cs and Sherry stayed with me. The bell rang, and Harriet's group stormed off, but Maria came back to me in the hall, and said she was with us. She was just scared of Harriet and the other girls."

"I can't blame her," I said.

"Yeah, then at lunch, Emma delivered a note to me that said we had until the end of lunch to join their new group, HAZE, and if we weren't with them, we were *nowhere*. So I held a meeting at the baseball diamond, read the note out to my girls, and gave them a choice. Luckily, they all decided to stay. We're calling ourselves the Six Queens. Our motto is All Equal, All Queens."

"Nice," I said. "On all counts."

"Thanks, but it's not like it's finished or anything," she said. "HAZE is going to be a serious problem." She sighed. "I just want the Magnas back like they were. So, what happened with Clouds? I heard he made a speech about the students revolting against the new rules."

"Yeah," I said. "He did."

I was surprised she didn't know more.

"We've got to do something about Clouds," she said. "He's been acting really weird, all secretive and snapping at everyone. Talk about being a tyrant!"

"Yeah, I guess," I said.

"And I think he's totally intimidated by you."

"What're you talking about, intimidated by me?"

"We've already talked about this, Chris," she said, "at Alfredo's. First, he left you out of Code: Get Nixon, and now every time you try to do something or say something, he either gets in your way or says you screwed up."

I thought this through. "Then why did he ask me to join in the first place?"

"I was thinking about that," she said. "Do you re-member the second meeting at the backstop when we all agreed to start the Revolutionists?"

"Um, yeah."

"Well, when you said you were in, he said, 'Better to have you with me than against me' or something like that?"

"He did?"

"Yep."

There was an awkward pause.

"So," I said, "are you . . . um . . . doing to the Ten Mile Skate this year?"

"Um . . . yeah," she said. "I think so. You?"

"Not sure," I said.

"Hey," she said, and paused. "Chris?"

"Yeah?"

There was silence, and then, she said, "Nothing. I'll see you tomorrow."

21

I hurried toward a large crowd at the basketball court the next morning, and I fought through to the front. It was ten minutes before the morning bell and Clouds wasn't there, but there was a new crate with red cloth draped over it like a presidential podium. Suddenly, Landry broke through the crowd, his long arms pushing everybody back.

"Give him space, people! Give him space!"

When I finally caught sight of Clouds, I was shocked.

He was wearing a black velvety cape that dragged along the snowy ground. He wore a top hat, with tufts of his fiery hair sticking out from underneath it. Clouds stepped up onto the crate and looked around at the crowd, his eyes blazing. He put his hand up and there was instant silence.

"Power to the students," he said.

He said it again, and this time all the students echoed in an eerie whisper, "Power to the students."

A chill ran down my spine. I looked over my shoulder and stood on my tiptoes. Where was the teacher on duty? This was scaring me.

"Yes," he said, clearing his throat. "You know what I

have to say! You know why you are gathered here today! You see that it's nothing strange! You see that it's time for change!" He paused and received soft, but enthusiastic applause. Clouds waited until there was silence again. "Enough talk—let's get down to business. As Lenon said, 'History will not forgive us if we don't assume power now.'"

He raised his fist.

"So, as an Act of Dissent against the Penguin's new school rules . . . *we will break them*."

The crowd murmured. I could see that Clouds was seriously under a spell—the spell of power—and it didn't look like anyone was around to stop him. Clouds's Act of Dissent was seriously going too far.

"How can they punish us if we *all* break the rules?" he demanded, throwing his arms up in the air.

"Yeah, seriously! Down with the new rules!" someone cried behind me. "Down with the new rules! Down with the new rules! Down with the new rules!"

A soft chant began, but Clouds waved his hands for everyone to hush.

"Okay, okay," he said. "Let's focus. Here's the plan. Are you with me?"

"Yes," the crowd replied.

"Now, people, listen to all the instructions first, and then begin," Clouds said.

I shook my head—he sounded like Mrs. Topper.

"Eighth graders will have a snowball fight on the soccer field. Seventh graders, it's time to build snow forts in
the gully—lots of them. Fifth and sixth graders, it's time
for a bathroom break. All of you head to the hallways." He
paused. "Okay! It's time for *revolution*!"

I watched in amazement as the crowd dispersed into
three distinct groups. The snowball fight got started right
away, as the older students made snowballs on their way
to the field. In minutes, tens of seventh graders were on
their knees by the gully building snow blocks. Then small
groups of younger students trickled in through the school
doors, and no one was coming back out. I stood on the
basketball court, tense and frozen to the spot. It was like
waiting for a balloon to pop.

Clouds remained on the podium, watching his revolution with glee. The two of us were the only ones left
on the basketball court. All of a sudden, Clouds glanced
toward the school and I turned to see what he was looking at. The Penguin was fighting through the current of
incoming youngsters, and heading toward the podium.
Landry, who had caught sight of the principal from the
field, was rushing toward Clouds. Clouds jumped down
and started to run toward the gully as Landry caught up
and followed closely behind.

Clouds's hat fell off, and as he looked back, he tripped,
his cape floating down like a net to engulf him. Landry,
who was following too closely behind, fell over Clouds

at full speed. They struggled for a while trying to disentangle themselves, and finally, with a thrust of his arms, Clouds broke free and got to his feet.

Clouds looked back at the Penguin, and then started to run again. He hadn't noticed that his cape had spun around to his front. The tip of his right boot caught a corner of his long cape, and Clouds tumbled back down to the ground.

In seconds, the Penguin was standing over him.

"I've got you now, Clouds McFadden," he said, gasping for breath. "Now up on your feet." He smiled. "You know exactly what's in store for you, don't you?"

Clouds shrugged, still on his knees. Landry was standing behind the Penguin, speechless. I watched Clouds slowly get up and give Landry a wink. Landry seemed to understand and moved off toward the gully. Clouds brushed off his black pants until his second in command had completely disappeared. Then he smiled at the Penguin. "Please . . . *sir* . . . lead the way."

As he walked by, Clouds looked in my direction, but it was like he didn't even see me.

When I got to class, I knew the best thing to do was put my head down and work, but I couldn't concentrate. It took Mrs. Topper fifteen minutes to get the class completely settled down, and then she made us work in complete silence until lunchtime.

Just before the bell, the Penguin knocked on the classroom door and ushered in Clouds, who went straight to his desk, grabbed a whole bunch of books in his arms, and went back to join the principal at the front of the class. He didn't look at anyone. The Penguin whispered to Mrs. Topper, then guided Clouds out of the classroom.

A minute later, the bell rang and students jumped out of their seats.

"Everyone stay seated," Mrs. Topper said.

We all groaned and slumped back into our seats.

"I just have a couple things to say," she said. "The first thing you should know is that Clouds McFadden has been suspended."

There was a class gasp.

"The second thing is that anyone with information about what happened today should speak with the principal at lunch hour."

I did not head to the principal's office at lunch, but I did walk out to the field so as to stay away from the other Revolutionists . . . and trouble. No luck. When I got to the far side of the field, I saw *all ten* former Magnas having an argument. My curiosity got the better of me and I angled slightly toward them. I was right: the Six Queens and HAZE were having a seriously heated discussion. Harriet was holding court confronting the Six Queens—specifically Carina.

"Carina," Harriet said, "didn't you tell me you were

sick of listening to Susan's promises of 'better times' on the school grounds?"

"Well, not exact—"

"Listen, you three," Harriet interrupted impatiently. "The sooner you realize you are going nowhere with Miss Goody Two-shoes over there, the sooner you'll start being popular again and having some fun. *Six Queens*—how stupid is *that* name?"

Susan lurched forward desperately. "Harriet, just stop—"

I moved in to help her.

"Oh, look," Harriet exclaimed, nudging Alita and completely ignoring Susan's plea. "It's Chris. What do you think, Mr. Nice Guy? Would you rather have fun with us or belong to Susan's Student Council Bore Sessions?"

Before I could say a thing, Alita jumped in. "You see? Not even her so-called *friends* will help her."

I glanced at Susan, who was looking desperately at her allies. Sherry was firmly by her side, as was Maria, but the Three Cs seemed to be wavering.

"Come on, Queens," Susan said. "This is exactly the kind of attitude—"

"Oh, no," Harriet interrupted again, in mock fear. "Mr. Meditation is coming over to save the damsel in distress."

It was true. Boris and his group, who I heard were calling themselves the Great Souls, were heading our way across the field. There were four of them in total, and they all had their heads shaved—Boris's was newly shorn—and wore brown cloaks that looked like cut-out sheets. Boris led the group, his long cloak dragging on the snow.

"Ladies, ladies," Boris said. "As . . . um . . . someone famous once said, 'Can't we all just get along?'"

"Sure," Emma said, leaping forward and leaning in close to him. "Get along, as in get lost. Now!"

Zigi taunted, "Why can't we all just get along, Boris? *You* tell us," while the rest kicked snow at him.

Without knowing I was even doing it, I shoved my way through the circle in front of Susan, and yelled, "Stop right now!"

The HAZE girls were stunned for a moment, and I looked around to see why this fight was escaping teacher supervision. Mrs. Crespin was the teacher on duty, but she was barking at Landry about something at the other end of the school grounds.

"You guys totally suck!" Susan said, behind me.

The Three Cs, sensing the sway of power was back with Susan, slipped quietly in behind her with Sherry and Maria.

Susan spoke again in a calm voice. "If you think my Six Queens would ever be involved in such a mean, horrible group, well, then, you've got another thing coming. I can't even believe we've destroyed the Magnas like this and—"

The bell cut off Susan's words. Harriet looked toward the school, shrugged, and then waved the rest to follow her to class. Susan then nodded to her Queens and they began to trail slowly behind their adversaries. As she passed me by, Susan mouthed "thanks," and I smiled back. I helped Boris brush the snow from his cloak and we all walked back to resume the school day.

Inside, the trouble to deal with was educational. The students in Mrs. Topper's class were working harder than anyone else in the school, and some were beginning to suggest—very angrily and audibly—that maybe taking Mrs. Topper's notes off the board wasn't such a bad thing after all. Mrs. Topper silenced the dissenters with a threat of working through break, so we were all heads-down when our teacher announced that she had to go to the office for a moment.

"Stay in your seats," she said, looking around at the usual suspects, "or *else*."

As soon as she was gone, Landry got up, walked across the front of the room, and strode up to Boris. He whispered something. Then he came down my aisle. As he passed, he leaned over and said, "Revolution . . . Saturday at three."

Just then Mrs. Topper came back into the room.

"What are you doing out of your seat, Landry?"

"I needed to borrow a pencil," he said, blinking his eyes innocently.

"Chris," she asked, "is this true?"

"Um, yeah," I said, shrugging. "But I don't have one."

"Landry Colburn," she said, irritated, "come here, and I'll lend you a pencil, but when I say 'Stay in your seat,' I mean it."

"Okay, Mrs. Topper," Landry said, turning and winking at me. But Landry's Code: Get Nixon success was now just barely keeping him out of trouble.

22

I stood leaning against the tree in Sterling Woods, waiting for everyone to arrive for the meeting. I heard a twig snap to my left, and I saw a cloaked figure drift from one tree to another in the distance. At first I thought it was Boris in his robe, but the cloak was black and velvety, not brown. It was Clouds.

Friday without Clouds at school had been very quiet, and the rest of us simply tried to stay out of trouble. At home, it was the same—I was careful and quiet. Nothing mattered now, except this three o'clock meeting.

"Hey, man," Clouds said as he approached, giving me one of his hearty shoulder slaps. "Everything is going as planned. I've started my revolution and only got a day of suspension for it."

"What do you mean *only* one day?"

"A little exile never hurt anyone, especially Lenon. I've got the Penguin right where I want him." He pounded his fist in his palm. "History must be repeated."

"I don't get it," I said. "Clouds, you're starting to sound like a tyrant yourself."

Clouds glared at me when we heard the crunching of footsteps from the direction of the road. It was Susan.

Boris chugged along behind her, red-faced and frantic. Closely behind Boris was Landry, who was wielding a branch and waving it playfully at Boris's legs.

"Nonviolence? You want nonviolence?" Landry shouted maniacally. He whipped the stick at Boris's legs. "I'll show you nonviolence."

"Stop, you beast!" Boris gasped desperately, his empty-lunged rasp barely audible.

"Clouds!" Landry exclaimed. "The Man is back in action!"

"You bet, Lan," he said, winking at him.

"Sure, Clouds," Susan said, sounding tired and even a bit irritated. "But haven't you taken this thing a little too far? And how did you escape from home?"

"The one thing I've learned over the last seventy-two hours," he snapped, "is that *real* change only comes by *force*."

"What about *peaceful* Acts of Dissent, like mine?" Boris demanded.

"It's all sweet and nice to make peaceful Acts of Dissent and have an eensie weensie bit of change," Clouds said, "but at the end of the day, Boris, Mrs. Topper is still totally in charge and we're working our brains off."

"I don't want her to *not* be in charge," Boris said. "I just want a better education."

"Well that's maybe why you aren't a *real* revolutionary leader," Clouds said, as Landry snickered.

Boris was speechless for once, just staring at Clouds in disbelief.

Clouds stepped forward and looked around at all of us. "Lenon said we need 'power based directly on force, unrestricted by any laws.' That's why I'm going after the new rules first. Then I'll go after the leader."

"Yeah!" Landry declared. "The Penguin is going down."

"But I still don't get it," I said. "Even if the Penguin does go down—whatever that means—then wouldn't you just become like another tyr—?"

"Chris," Clouds interrupted, "do your research first, please, before you question my authority. Have you done your research?"

"You mean about Lenon? No, but—"

"That's what I thought," he said, turning from me. "Moving on . . . I've decided I'm going to enlist a team of guys. I'm going to start with some muscle, and hire Terrence as my chief. Then I'll get him to recruit some *real* power and—"

"What are you talking about, Clouds?" Susan interrupted, trembling with anger.

Clouds's face burned red. "I would appreciate it if you didn't call me Clouds—it's Vladimir from now on."

"Well, I don't care what you want me to call you!" Susan said, almost yelling.

The rest of us took uneasy steps backward.

"You have no idea what we've been going through," she continued, her eyes welling. "Well . . . what *I've* been going through with HAZE and the Six Queens. And NOW you start telling us that real power is about hiring bullies?"

Boris jumped in. "The Great Souls have been busy trying to stop the kind of violence you are talking about. I am fully against hiring bullies because—"

"Listen, we don't want to hear about it, Gandhi," Landry sneered. "Right, Vlads?"

Clouds nodded, but he was still glaring at Susan. Then he turned to me. "What do *you* say, Chris? Are you with me or not?"

Susan looked up at me as Boris turned his gaze to the heavens. Landry was bulging his eyes at me.

I looked at Clouds.

"No," I said. "It's wrong, Clouds—I mean, Vladimir or whatever. I mean it's not fair—"

"Traitor," he said. "I'm only interested in real revolutionaries like the French Jacobins. You're no better than that softie, Lafayette. I'm done here—with all of you moderates. Let's go, Lan!"

He turned and calmly walked away in the direction from which he'd come.

Landry hesitated for a moment. "You guys are crazy," he said and then ran after Clouds.

The three of us stood still.

"What the heck is going on with Clouds?" Susan said, grabbing her head with both hands.

"I have no idea," Boris said, shaking his head. "The

power has gotten to him. Clouds has completely gone off the deep end. I mean, we're all allowed to change a little"—he paused to acknowledge his own changes with a rub of his shaven head and a whisk of his sheet robe—"but this is going way overboard! I'm with you, Chris, but I've got to reconsider this whole Revolutionist thing. Gandhi was shot dead, after all, by an extremist who thought he wasn't going far enough." He paused. "Maybe we should all stop it with this history business . . ." He turned and trudged away toward the road. "Later, guys."

Susan didn't move. She just stared at the snowy ground. I felt like I should say something consoling, feeling the need for some support myself.

"You all right?" I asked cautiously.

Susan lifted her head and smiled weakly. "Yeah, I guess."

I scanned the dreary forest. We were completely alone.

"Hey," I said, "how about we go get a hot chocolate or something?"

"Yeah," she said, smiling. "That's a great idea. I really need a break from being a Queen . . . of any kind."

We walked to Trudy's Café, ordered a couple of hot chocolates, and sat down in a booth.

"By the way, thanks for saving me in the field this morning," Susan said. "It's not a lot of fun being me these days."

"Yeah, I noticed."

"I don't know what the heck is going on with Clouds," she said. "Talk about going back on *everything* he said before."

"Um," I said, taking a sip, "I thought you would have known what he was up to because, well, because you and Clouds, um—"

"Clouds and I what?"

"Well, because you were spending so much time together and because, well . . . aren't the two of you doing the Ten Mile Skate together tomorrow?"

"*What* are you talking about?" she demanded.

"I don't know," I said, defensively. "Harriet kind of implied that—"

"Ugh," she said, slapping her palm on her forehead, "and you listened to that liar?"

"Yeah, well," I said, taking another sip to find the right words. "You acted so weird when I asked you about it on the phone, and you and Clouds were always disappearing together . . . for a while there."

"Um . . . Hello, Chris?" she said. "Can we talk about reality now, please?"

I looked down, embarrassed.

"Okay, first of all," she said, her voice softer, "Clouds was my adviser, and that's why we were spending so much time together. He was helping me figure out what to do with the Magnas."

"Oh."

"But I *do* have something to tell you. Remember how I said I was trying to follow Queen Elizabeth's life very closely?"

"Uh-huh," I said, more confused than ever.

"And," she said, leaning forward, "how I told you that Elizabeth used marriage as a way of keeping other countries on England's side?"

"Yeah."

"And how she pretended to want to marry kings and princes from places like Spain and France so that they wouldn't attack England?"

I nodded, still perplexed.

"Anyway, I don't think you know Carina's brother, John, since he's a freshman—"

"What about him?" I said, my stomach dropping.

"Well, Carina told me that he wanted to go to the Ten Mile Skate with me, and so . . . so I kind of figured if I asked him, that maybe I could get the Three Cs on my side."

"Oh," I said.

"Yeah," she said, looking down. "So I had to, like, dump you, or whatever, so that Carina knew I was serious about him. But the really stressful part is I'm *not* serious about him at all. I really don't like him one bit."

"Well," I said, shrugging like I didn't care, "you know what Clouds said: 'History must be repeated.'"

"What? He said that?"

"Yep, just before everyone arrived at the meeting today."

"Hmm, that's so wrong," she said, looking out the window. She turned back to me. "After we talked at Alfredo's, I asked my grandma why she said history must *not* be repeated, and she told me that history is full of terrible meaningless wars, greed, and murder—mistakes we don't ever want to make again."

"But those are just the bad parts," I argued. "Maybe we're just repeating the good parts—like giving the students equality and power."

"Yeah, that's what I thought too, but then I realized that we aren't exactly struggling at Laverton Middle School. We're getting a good education, for gosh sakes. And things are pretty fair in our lives, even though it doesn't always seem that way. And you know, maybe following in Elizabeth's shoes to get the Magnas back on track wasn't the best idea. She wasn't exactly the nicest queen of all time. She sent people to the tower." Susan slid her finger across her throat, and then frowned. "If *that's* repeating history, I'd rather not be a part of it."

"I hear you," I said, nodding. Then something struck me. "Wait! You're a queen . . . and I saved you from HAZE!"

"What are you talking about, Chris?"

"My own research. What happened today on the field was just like with Lafayette's life," I said, my eyes wide.

"He saved the queen, the French one, from a furious crowd, just like I did with you and HAZE. You know . . . I think maybe history *is* sort of repeating."

"I don't know about that," Susan said, grabbing her coat and taking a large swallow of hot chocolate. "It must have been in your subconscious or something. Maybe we should just focus on our own modern-day problems, don't you think? Like for example, if any of the girls see us here, I'm totally dead! I'll lose the Three Cs, and then the Six Queens, and the Magnas will be done for."

I grabbed my coat as well and followed her outside.

"Wait a sec," I said, stopping her on the sidewalk. "We've still got to figure out what's going on with Clouds and stop him."

"Yeah, I know. But that's *your* modern-day problem, Chris, because I've got my hands full with the nastiest group of girls as my archenemies, a flaky set of allies, and a jerk to skate ten long miles with. Meanwhile Boris is in La La Land and Landry's on Planet Vladimir." She leaned over and gave me a hug. "And I've really really gotta go."

I wasn't expecting a hug.

She pulled away and smiled. "Talk to you later, Chris. Good luck."

"All right, Crick," Mom said, at the dinner table on Sunday night. "We've had just about enough of this silence bit.

You've been way too quiet all weekend long. Tell us what's going on. Now."

When Mom used this voice, it meant trouble. Even Dad was silent and still. Little did Mom know, my silence was now from heart-thumping exhilaration. I was still celebrating the hug and smile Susan had given me.

I sat up in my seat. "Um, well, it's really noth—"

"Don't give me that 'it's nothing' business. I know my son. Something is going on."

I put my fingers on my temples. How could I explain?

"Well," I said, with no idea of what I was going to say, "when, um, Clouds came into our class a month ago, it was like he took me out of this, like, terrible slump or something, and I felt suddenly great and, like, alive, and happy . . . but, now things have suddenly gotten really, really complicated."

"What kind of complicated?" Mom said, leaning forward.

"Um, the kind of complicated that's too hard to explain?" I suggested.

"Hmm," she said. "Does this complicated have anything to do with the Magnas?"

"The Magnas?" I said, sitting back, totally shocked. I had to think quickly. "Sort of. Why?"

"The Magnas are very secret," she said, ignoring my question. "You shouldn't know *anything* about them."

"Um, yeah," I said. "That's . . . very true."

"Christopher David Stren," Mom said, throwing down her napkin. "If you don't tell me what's going on, you are grounded every weekend from now until spring break."

I looked at her and then down at my plate. More than a month's worth of freedom was at stake. This was no time to give in.

"Fine," I said, "Can I be excused then?"

There was silence as my parents stared at each other, and then Mom said, "Suit yourself. But you are not leaving your room for the rest of the night."

"Okay," I said, and cleared my dishes.

I grabbed the "E" and "L" volumes of the encyclopedia, and went up the ladder to my room.

I sat at my desk, and began reading about Queen Elizabeth. It said that when Elizabeth was young, she was imprisoned in the Tower of London, and thought she might be executed by her sister, the then-queen, Mary, for not being a Catholic; Elizabeth was a Protestant, which seemed to matter a lot in those days. When Elizabeth finally became queen, she brought the country from very bad times to very good times. Soon the country began winning wars, the economy started to run well, and people were living better lives.

I also found something that made me think. Elizabeth had a very close friend throughout her life named Robert Dudley. Not William Cecil, her political adviser, but a real best friend. Dudley and Elizabeth were inseparable for the years before she became Queen and, once she was crowned, Elizabeth continued to treat him specially. People thought that the two were in love, but Elizabeth would not get married, for strategic reasons. Finally Elizabeth turned on Dudley, saying, 'I would rather be a beggar and single than a Queen and married.' They were never close again.

My mind began to race. If history *was* repeating, who was this Robert Dudley guy supposed to be? Me? Who said I wanted to be used like a pawn, and then dumped like peasant? Whoever said I liked Susan in the first place? My mind was made up: this history would not—could not—repeat.

I closed the book and went to the "L" volume, and found where I left off with Lafayette. I scanned for the Jacobins. When I found them, I didn't like what I saw. They wanted a Republic for the French people, and they definitely didn't want a King. The Jacobins were willing to do *anything* to get rid of him. Lafayette wanted less power for King Louis, but he didn't want him taken out. Finally, Lafayette agreed to lead the army to protect the King, and the Jacobins declared Lafayette a traitor. Exactly what Clouds called me today! Then the Jacobins chopped Louis's head off in a guillotine, and executed anyone who opposed them. And this was who Clouds thought were the best?

Then I remembered my Assembly resolution. I hadn't

thought of it in days, and I wondered where it might be. The bottom of Landry's bag, I guessed, or perhaps destroyed in one of Boris's peace missions. Susan hadn't mentioned receiving the resolution so I guessed it was lost. Maybe Clouds had destroyed it. It didn't seem unrealistic. All the more reason to do *this* research and stop him.

I flipped through from the back of the book and tried to find Lenon. I found *Lens*, as in glasses and eyes; *Lenoir, Etienne*, who invented the first internal combustion engine in the 1800s; *Lennon, John*, the peaceful ex-Beatle who was shot in 1980; *Lennox, Countess Margaret Douglas*, a countess from Elizabeth's day who was imprisoned in the Tower of London for murder. But *Lenon* was nowhere to be found. I searched for a couple of frustrated minutes over the same few pages. Where was Lenon? Was this all some trick? I was just about to close the volume when the word *revolution* caught my eye. It was under the heading *Leninism*. I flipped back a few pages. I couldn't believe what I saw.

There was Lenon, but he wasn't spelled that way. The actual spelling was *L-E-N-I-N*—Clouds always said that spelling was stupid, but this proved how important it really was. My eyes darted over the pages and my heart pounded—I felt like I was finding the secret combination to a lock.

Vladimir Lenin *was* a revolutionary leader of Russia in the early twentieth century. He started a political movement against the all-powerful czar, just as Clouds had told us. He led a group that was called the Bolsheviks, who spoke publicly against the royalty because they were tyrants and needed to be stopped. Lenin was so outspoken about equality for all people that he was exiled by Russian authorities. After years in exile in Europe, he returned to lead the revolution.

This sounded familiar. Clouds was suspended for a day, and was starting his own revolution.

There was more. When Lenin got to back Russia in 1917, he soon gained control of the government. The problem was that Lenin ended up being a tyrant himself. They called his reign the Red Terror because he used brute force to stop anyone who was against him. He even had people *killed*. This was beginning to sound way too scary.

I slammed the book shut. Lafayette or not, traitor or not, I had to do something.

• PART 5 •
Will the Real Leader
Please Stand Up?

23

I turned on some music so that my parents couldn't hear me, picked up the phone, and dialed Susan's number.

"Hello?" she answered.

"Suz," I whispered. "Something crazy is going on. Lenin isn't Lenon!"

"What are you talking about? And why are you whispering?"

"Clouds is Lenin, but it's not spelled that way!"

"What way? What's going on? Are you all right, Chris?"

"Yes, of course," I said, still keeping my voice down. "It's just that—"

"Wait—my mom," she said, putting the phone down. She returned in seconds. "I have to go, Chris. Sorry. My grandma just arrived."

"It's okay," I said. "I have to go, too. Just tell your grandma that history will not be repeated."

Susan giggled. "Okay, if you insist."

"We need to meet tomorrow—tomorrow morning at eight, at the tree."

"What about Boris?" she asked.

"I'll call him," I said.

"Okay, see you tomorrow."

As soon as I hung up with Susan, I punched in Boris's number. His mother answered.

"Hello, Mrs. Bergman," I said, cupping my mouth so that the sound wouldn't carry. "It's Chris Stren. Is Boris there, please?"

"I'm sorry, Chris. He can't come to the phone."

I thought for a second.

"Mrs. Bergman"— I had to go for flattery—"I, um, have . . . a homework problem, and I know Boris is the one guy who will know the answer."

There was a pause.

"Yes, yes," she said, considering. "He probably is your best bet. Okay, Chris, he can speak to you for a *minute*."

I heard her call out to Boris.

After a couple of seconds, there was mumbled discussion between Boris and his mother, and then he spoke tentatively in the receiver. "Chris?"

"Sorry about that, Boris. Listen, I just found out something crazy, so Susan and I need you to meet us at eight tomorrow morning in the usual spot."

There was silence on the line. "What kind of crazy are we talking about?"

"Clouds crazy."

Boris paused and then finally said, "This better be good. I'll do my best, but I can't promise anything."

I hung up and fell onto my couch. My heart was still beating rapidly, and I was scared. Susan, Boris, and I had to find away to stop Clouds before things got even more out of hand.

24

"T his *really* better be good," Boris complained as I arrived at the tree on Monday morning. "What's the deal?"

Both he and Susan were already waiting for me there.

"Okay, guys, I finally did the research, and it's spelled L-e-n-*I*-n!" I said, holding up the encyclopedia. "And we're in trouble."

"I forgot Clouds was such a bad speller!" Boris said, giving the side of his stubbly head a whack. "I guess I got sidetracked with Gandhi."

"It doesn't matter," I said. "We can do our work now. Do you want to read, or should I explain?"

"Chris, you're freaking me out," Susan said. "What's so bad about Clouds and Lenin?"

"Okay . . . Vladimir Lenin was the leader of this party called the Bolsheviks, who took control of the government in Russia. He started with good ideas, like equality for everyone, but then he ended up being a terrible tyrant himself."

"Hello? That sounds familiar!" Susan exclaimed.

"But that's not the worst of it," I said. "When he started

this Red Terror thing, he was taking down anyone that got in his way, as in he had people *killed*."

"That's terrible," she said. "But I'm sure Clouds isn't going to kill anyone. I *am* worried this whole power thing has really gotten to his head. I've seen it before with Harriet, and it isn't pretty."

"We must stop him, I agree," Boris stated. "But peacefully."

"Yeah," I said. "Peacefully, but not passively. We need to go right at him, and remind him of where we started . . . where he *got* us started."

"I agree," Susan said, nodding. "And I don't think we should wait. As soon as we get to school, let's just walk right up and confront him. No more sneaking around."

"I don't know," Boris said.

"I think you're right, Susan," I said. "He won't be expecting it."

"Okay," Boris said. "But don't say I didn't warn you two."

"Positive, Boris," I repeated. "Think positive."

"Positive, peaceful, but not passive," Boris said, shrugging. "It's not exactly Satyagraha, but then again, I'm not exactly Gandhi."

When we got to the school grounds, it wasn't hard to find Clouds. It looked as though he had already recruited his muscle guys—Terrence and a bully from Susan's class,

Bobbie Mowers, were standing on either side of him. We strode silently toward them. Landry was nowhere to be seen.

"What do you want?" Terrence said, stepping forward.

"Clouds, this is crazy," I said, stopping and talking around Terrence. "I did my research—we know who Lenin is and we know you are heading for trouble."

Clouds just smirked.

"What do you want us to do, Vladimir?" Terrence said, turning to him.

"Vladimir?!" Boris exclaimed. "This is crazy, Clouds. It's all gone too far. I'll lose the robe and cut it with the Gandhi stuff, just *stop this craziness*. You can't be Lenin. You are going to get yourself in trouble and—"

Clouds raised his right hand. Terrence and Bobbie nodded, grabbed Boris, and began dragging him away.

"Look, Clouds!" I said, taking a step forward. "You don't make change by bullying and force. You are just going to get in more trouble, and then you'll be expelled."

"Yeah, Clouds," Susan said. "We're on your side. In the student council meeting yesterday, I suggested we take a good look at the new school rules to make sure they are fair."

Clouds's eyes went wide. "I knew it. I *knew* it. As soon as I leave the country for a while, you Mensheviks try to take part in government and take the power away from the People. There's no halfway about this, comrades. The new rules have got to go."

"Aren't you going a little too far with all this?" Susan asked.

"Ha, that's a funny one," Clouds laughed derisively. "You sound like my mother."

An idea hit me. I took a deep breath.

"I didn't want to mention your mom, Clouds," I said, "but do you remember the conversation I overheard the other day in my attic?"

"You keep your mouth shut," Clouds sneered, stepping forward menacingly.

My heart was pounding in my chest when I heard Terrence say behind me, "Vladimir, Mr. McNally is coming our way."

Clouds glared at me and strode away, leading his thugs toward the gully.

Susan and I watched as they disappeared.

"Well, that didn't work," she said, shaking her head as Boris stumbled back to us. "What happened with his mom?"

"Um," I said. "It's nothing. I'll tell you later."

"What's going on, kids?" Mr. McNally said from a few feet behind us. "Were those boys causing you any trouble?"

"No," I said. "Not at all. We were just having a talk."

* * *

I couldn't concentrate during class, so I took out a piece of paper. I looked over at Clouds, who was playing it cool, listening to Mrs. Topper, and doing his work. I started to write a note:

> Hey Clouds,
>
> I was just thinking about our first meeting at the baseball diamond and how amazing it felt to finally do something worthwhile and exciting. I'd never felt better in my life. What's gone wrong? Remember how we were going to stop the tyrants at school? Haven't you become a tyrant yourself by bossing people around and hiring bullies? Maybe it wasn't such a great idea to follow these leaders and revolutionists. It's dangerous to repeat history, especially Lenin's. You are heading for serious trouble.
>
> Anyway, sorry about mentioning your mom, but there's nothing wrong with following your parents' rules.
>
> Your pal,
> Chris

At break time, I walked straight over to Clouds and his mob by the snow forts. Landry stepped away from the others to confront me.

"I've got something for Clouds," I said.

"You mean Vladimir?"

I rolled my eyes with disgust. "No, I mean Clouds!"

Landry smirked and turned around to Clouds, Terrence, and Bobbie. "Anyone know a Clouds? This guy's got something for someone called Clouds."

"Take it and tell him to get lost," Clouds said.

"Thanks for nothing, Landry," I said, turning my face away.

"You're welcome," Landry said, grabbing the note from my hand and heading back toward the snow forts.

I stood there for a moment, and then looked around. The Queens and HAZE were glaring at each other from their separate camps. Boris was back with his Great Souls, but their robes were gone. When the bell finally rang, I went into the school and stopped by my locker to grab a book. A note dropped to the floor. It was my letter, but red pen was scribbled over it. It read:

Mention my mom again, and you will have serious trouble.

V.L.

I ripped up the note and stuffed it in my pocket. How was I going to get through to Clouds? As I closed my locker door and headed back to class, an idea, a last ditch attempt, popped into my head.

* * *

"Hey, easy, man!" Landry said, as I stepped in front of him in the hallway at the end of the day. Mrs. Topper had kept him in for a couple of minutes after class; the latest chink in Code: Get Nixon's armor. "Is this some kind of ambush or something? Aren't you supposed to say stick 'em up? That's no gun." He pointed at the encyclopedia in my hand. "What? You going to threaten me with a book?"

I held up the "L" volume and whispered, "Listen, Landry. We found Lenin. Clouds was spelling it wrong. He's following this tyrant's life almost exactly, and it doesn't look good. He's leading you into serious trouble. You've got to read this." I thrust the book toward him, but he slapped it to the ground.

"I'm not going to read some stupid book," he said. "Vlads is the Man and I'm his Second in Command. And we are after *real* power. You don't get it. He says that once he gets power at school, it will be peaceful and he will make everyone equal and happy. He says—"

"Landry," I said, still holding the book out, "if you'll just read this you'll see that it's not exactly going to happen that way. Lenin had the best intentions for the Russian people, too, but ended up being bad."

"What? Did he, like, blow someone's brains up?" Landry joked nervously.

"He ordered his enemies to death and to prison camps and—"

"You don't know what you're talking about," Landry said. "I'm not going to read some idiotic encyclopedia, and I'm definitely not going to listen to you. So stay away from us, and you'll be just fine, Chris. Just like Vlads said, you're like Lafayette. You could never handle any *real* revolution in the first place."

"I'm not Lafayette, Landry, and Clouds isn't Lenin!" I exclaimed. "We are eighth-grade students at Laverton Middle School, and compared to the Penguin, Mrs. Topper, and all the teachers, Clouds is the worst tyrant."

Landry smirked and walked away. I needed to figure out how to topple the new tyrant in our midst.

Okay, class," Mrs. Topper said the next morning. "Please hand in your space essays. And remember, your Viking assignments are due at the end of the week."

My projects! I had completely forgotten about them. I had some of the work done, but the most of it was at home, and I wasn't close to being ready to hand it in. I bent down, pretending to get my project, and tried to avoid Mrs. Topper's gaze, but it was no use. She looked right at me and said, "Did anyone not hand in his or her project?"

I slowly put up my hand.

"Chris," she said, "very disappointing. Everyone get to work on your Viking projects. Chris, speak to me at break."

I worked hard until break hoping this would help my cause. When the bell rang, I waited until everyone had left. Mrs. Topper finally got up and walked to the back of the classroom. She leaned against the desk in front of me.

"Chris," she said, crossing her arms. "I thought after my talk with your mother that things were going to get better. But I've noticed you've been even more distracted recently. Is everything okay?"

"Um . . . yes," I replied.

"Do you have a sound excuse for not handing in your work?"

I thought for a second. Explaining it all would take a month.

"No," I said. "But I can hand in my assignment tomorrow."

"Fine," she said, "but that's not good enough, and you know it." She sighed. "You can go."

When I got outside, Clouds was standing with HAZE at the basketball court, with Terrence and Bobbie nearby. Harriet was talking to him and she was pointing toward the Six Queens at the baseball backstop. I had a flashback to Clouds's first day at school: he had gone right up to the Magnas—to Harriet!—and said that if they ever needed his *assistance*, he would be willing to help. Was it now actually happening? Had he planned this all along? I had no idea what the two tyrants were scheming, but I was scared for Susan. I flew down the steps and headed straight toward the Six Queens, who were all watching.

"Hey," I said to Susan as I approached. She didn't answer.

"Hey. I said, 'Hey!'"

Susan's eyes shifted, but she was looking right through me. "Sir Babington. Talk about doing your research. I can't believe it . . . It's just like Sir Babington."

Sir Babington. I had never heard the name before—or

had I? Was she calling me the name of that pathetic guy who waited around to get married to Queen Elizabeth? I wasn't sure, but I couldn't help my face from flushing angrily.

"I'm not Sir Babington," I said, "because history is *not* repeating."

"No, no," Susan said, in a daze. "Not you . . ."

"Who's Sir Babington?" Catia said, from behind. "What's going on?

"No one," Susan said, turning. "Nothing."

"Exactly," I snapped. "That's why I'm not him, and I'm out of here."

"No," Susan said. "Wait—"

"Whatever," I said, and stormed back toward the school.

"Your teacher called at lunchtime," Mom said, after school. I dropped my bag and sat at the kitchen table.

"What'd she say?" I said, glumly.

"She said you didn't hand in an assignment today. You know what that means, don't you?"

"Yep," I said, resigned. "I'm grounded."

"Well," she said. "Not unless you can give me an explanation."

"Okay, well," I said, thinking. "Well . . . you know how, like, we had that group?"

"Yes."

"Well, it's kind of gotten out of control, and some of us are trying to stop history repeating. But everyone else is wrapped up with other stuff, so it's like my responsibility to figure it out . . . except I can't."

"I have no idea what you are talking about," Mom said, exasperated, sitting down. She looked to the ceiling and sighed. "Is this about Clouds? I finally met his mother in the grocery store. She seems to have her hands full with that son of hers."

My mind was spinning. I looked at the wall in a daze. My heart began to race.

"I've got to ask the biggest favor," I said, pleading.

"You are not in the position to ask for any favors, Chris."

"I know, I know, but it's the last one, I promise," I pleaded. "I just *have* to use the phone up in my room. I'll work all night, and things will be much better very very soon."

"*What* is going on?"

"I'm not exactly sure," I said. "But I think I might have an idea. I promise I'll explain it all when I do." I paused and looked her in the eyes. "It's really really really important that I do this . . . *myself.*"

She looked up to the ceiling again and put her hand on her forehead.

"I should start calling myself Mrs. Pushover," she said. "Okay . . . *one* two-minute phone call, and then down here with your books. I'll give you a chance to work things out, but if I don't find out what's going on soon I'm going to start calling parents."

I got up to my room and dialed.

"Hello?" I was in luck—it was Boris, not his mother.

"Hi. It's Chris," I said. "I've figured it out how to get to Clouds . . . I think."

"How?"

"I don't have time to explain. Do you have your tape recorder still?"

"I don't like where this is going," Boris answered. "But yes."

"Okay," I said. "I need to you get into an argument with Clouds tomorrow and get his voice on tape. Make him talk about Lenin, okay?"

"Like Nixon," Boris said, sounding a little excited. "Who are you going to play it for?"

"I can't tell you right now," I said. "I gotta get off the phone. I'm up to my eyeballs in trouble."

"Your space essay, right?" he said.

"Yep," I said, sighing. "I've got to get downstairs and finish it up. Get me the tape recorder with Clouds's voice as soon as you can tomorrow, and I think we'll put an end to all of this."

"Okay, Chris," he said, "I'll have to take your word for it."

"Yes," I said. "You will."

After I hung up the phone, I grabbed my schoolwork and went back downstairs. Mom was reading in the living room, so I cleared my mind as best I could and got down to writing my essay.

26

I got to school just before bell the next morning, as I was up late finishing my essay. When I got into class, I handed it in right away, and got a nod from Mrs. Topper. When I turned to the class, I glanced at Boris, who winked at me from his seat. Behind him, Clouds was eyeing me suspiciously, so I looked away. I went to my desk and got right down to work on my Viking project. When the break bell rang, I hung back a bit and then followed the class outside.

Boris wasn't wasting any time. He was already talking to Clouds on the field, his Great Souls at his side. I jumped down the stairs and got as close as I could get without drawing attention. I didn't hear what Boris said, but I caught a response from Clouds.

". . . and you're lucky the teacher on duty is close by, because there's only room for one kind of revolution around here, and it's not passive, it's aggressive. The Bolsheviks are the best. As soon as I help HAZE crush Queen Elizabeth's little empire today, the New Alliance is going after the Penguin."

It was February 1—Harriet was leader of the Magnas!

Boris threw his hands in the air. "But you told us—"

"I didn't tell you anything," seethed Clouds, now just inches from Boris's face. "You're blaming *me* for your bad haircut and pathetic passive resistance? Why don't you sit in a corner and go on a hunger strike? Maybe Mrs. Topper will hear your stomach grumble or something."

That was all I needed to hear. I looked across the field and saw Susan and her Six Queens in a huddle. Susan looked like she was preparing for battle. I started heading toward the school, when I heard a voice behind me.

"Chris."

I turned around. It was Doug.

"Yeah," I said.

"What's going on?"

"Not much," I said. "You?"

"Crazy stuff if you hadn't noticed. The Magnas have split up, that guy Clouds has started some gang with Terrence and Bobbie, and Susan's got this weird group called the Queens or something!"

"Oh really," I said, shrugging. "I hadn't noticed."

"Wake up, man," Doug said. "There's a whole world in front of your eyes."

"Yeah," I said, walking away. "Thanks for the update."

As soon as I was a good distance from Doug, Boris headed my way. His Great Souls were trailing behind him, but he stopped them with a hand.

"Chris," he said loudly, walking up and winking. "We've come to ask if you want to join Boris's Peace Brigade—no more Great Souls. Our new motto is No Robes, More Hair, and Way More Peace."

"Sounds . . . interesting," I said, laughing. "But I've got my own history to follow—I mean change."

Boris smiled. "I'm sorry you feel that way, but if you decide to change your mind, we'll be right here in the schoolyard."

He put his hand out to shake, and I could feel the cold recorder in my hand.

I went straight to the back entrance, where the pay phone was. I rewound the tape and listened once. I rewound again and then stopped at the perfect spot. I threw in a handful of quarters and punched in Clouds's dad's number.

After a couple of rings, a man finally answered.

"Hello?"

"Um, yes, is this Clouds's dad?"

"Yes, it is. Mike McFadden here. Who is this?"

"Hi, I'm a friend of Clouds's. It's Chris Stren. I slept on your couch the other night."

"Oh yes—Chris. I was sorry I wasn't awake to meet you in the morning—it'd been a long night. Clouds has spoken very highly of you. What's up?"

"Well, actually, there's a bit of a problem," I explained. "I know you don't believe in rules and tyrants and everything, but I think maybe Clouds has gone a bit overboard."

"Wait a second," he said, his voice going serious. "Who

said I don't believe in rules? This doesn't have anything to do with Clouds's suspension, does it?"

"Um . . . yes, sort of. But Clouds doesn't think he was suspended—he thinks he was exiled. Clouds actually thinks he's Vladimir Lenin."

"What do you mean?" he said, laughing. "Is this some joke?"

"No, really, not at all," I said. "I've got proof."

"Okay, Chris," he said. "Let's hear it then."

"Just listen," I said, putting the tape recorder to the receiver and pressing play.

"Who do you think you are?" Boris's crackly voice demanded.

"You know exactly who I am, Gandhi. I'm Vladimir Lenin, and I'm taking matters into my own hands with FORCE. It's the only way."

"But that's tyrannical, Clouds. Don't you get it? You've become what you were fighting against in the first place. Wake up, man!"

"If you'd done your research, Boris, you'd know that a leader has to—"

"But you misspelled Lenin. How were we supposed to know you messed up?"

"Come here and say that, Cueball, and I'll show you messed up."

I stopped the tape. "Hello?" I said.

"I'll be there as soon as I can," he said, and hung up the phone.

My heart was racing—it felt like it had been racing for days. Back in class, I tried to do my Viking work, but ended up just staring at my research. Finally the bell rang for lunch. I got out of my seat to go, but Mrs. Topper stopped me. "Chris, can you please stay behind?"

Clouds looked at me and smirked before he stepped out the door.

"Right then, Chris," Mrs. Topper said to me as she came up the aisle. "You weren't working all period long."

"Yes," I agreed, looking at the door. "I know . . . Sorry."

"You'd better show me much better effort going forward, Chris," she said.

"Yes, of course. Definitely. I will."

"You aren't really listening to me, are you, Chris?"

"No . . . I mean yes. I mean . . . I'm sorry. Really. I'm just a little distracted. I'll snap out of it soon, I promise, Mrs. Topper. So . . . um . . . can I go?"

She stared at me. "Okay. But I'm watching you, young man."

"Thanks," I said, getting up before she could say another word. I went through the classroom door, ran down the hallway, and burst through the school doors.

Clouds was arguing with Susan on the field, and it appeared as though he was winning the battle: the Cs were making their way toward HAZE on the basketball court. Then I saw Boris's Peace Brigade run interference; Boris had stopped the Three Cs in their tracks, but I knew he couldn't contain them peacefully for long. Then, out of the corner of my eye, I saw all four HAZE members move toward Boris and the Cs, with Harriet leading the way. Clouds and Susan also gravitated toward the rest. This wasn't history repeating—it was history being made.

I jumped down the steps and started running toward *everyone*. I ran as fast as I could, and was about halfway there when I heard someone yell behind me. I kept running, though—nothing was going to get in my way this time. But then I heard the voice again, and it sounded familiar. Something told me to slow down and stop, so I did. I turned. A man was running behind me. He was tall with short salt and pepper hair. He rushed by and then stopped in front of Boris, the Three Cs, HAZE, Susan, and Clouds.

"Clouds!" he said. "Come here, right now."

Clouds turned toward the man and froze.

"Dad! What are you doing here?" he asked, and then glanced back at me accusingly. I looked right back at him, unafraid.

"What's with this Lenin business I'm hearing about?"

"Oh that!" Clouds said, walking toward his dad. "I was just playing around really. I—"

"Clouds," his father said. "No more lies. The truth, please."

Clouds's face went red, and he looked to the ground. I heard more footsteps and turned, and the Penguin rushed past me.

"Excuse me, sir," he said, waddling up to them. "Who are you, please?"

The man cleared his throat. "My name is Mike McFadden. I am Clouds's father."

"Well," the Penguin said. "It's a pleasure to meet you, sir, but the rule here at Laverton Middle School is that parents or any visitors must sign in at the office first."

"Sorry, sorry," Mr. McFadden said, putting his hand to his head. "You are right. I wasn't thinking. Makes complete sense. For the safety of everyone . . . of course."

"That's right, Mr. McFadden," the Penguin said, nodding. "That's what all good rules are for."

The bell rang, and he waved Clouds and his father toward the school. Then he looked over his shoulder at everyone else. "The rest of you back to class *immediately*."

27

When I opened my locker a folded piece of paper fell to the ground. I bent down and sighed; this was likely another mean note from Clouds. I stuffed it in my pocket, as I didn't want to be late and get myself into more trouble with Mrs. Topper. But when I stepped into the classroom, Mrs. Topper was absent and the class was again abuzz with news of Clouds McFadden—his father's sudden arrival and its powerful effect on Clouds. At his seat, Landry hung his head and kept silent for once—his tyrannical leader had been toppled. I looked over at Boris, who grinned at me, pointed to Clouds's empty desk, and gave me the thumbs up: we had stopped Clouds and history from repeating. Somehow I didn't feel as good as I should have.

I found my seat and got my Viking research out. I looked down at the notes, but my eyes just wouldn't stay on the page. I gazed aimlessly around the room. Mrs. Topper still hadn't arrived—perhaps she was dealing with Clouds and his father at the office—and the rest of the class was still leaning across aisles and chatting. I remembered the note—I felt for it in my back pocket and pulled it out.

It wasn't a message from Clouds—it was my assembly resolution! The sheet was dog-eared and wrinkled, but six teachers had signed it! All this time the Revolutionists—at the least some of them—had been helping me. Boris had gotten Mr. Danforth to sign. I looked over at my fellow Revolutionist, but he was in his own world. Neither Mrs. Crespin's nor Mr. Singh's signature was there, which wasn't a surprise; Lenin and his second in command had been too wrapped up in revolution. But there were signatures from Mrs. Deercroft, Mr. McNally, and my fifth grade teacher, Mrs. Simpson. Susan had been even busier than I thought.

I needed to call a meeting. I stood up, but then had second thoughts and sat back down. I looked at the sheet for a moment. Then I folded it carefully, put it back in my pocket, and got down to work.

I went to the Penguin's office at the end of the day. He was leaning over some paperwork and didn't notice me. I knocked lightly on the door.

He lifted his head. "Yes?"

"Um, hi Mr. Dorfman. It's Chris Stren from Mrs. Topper's class. I have, um, I have something to talk to you about."

He looked back down at his work. "Chris, you can schedule a meeting with Mrs. DeSantis for tomorrow. You know the rules."

I didn't move. I looked down at my resolution, which was open in front of me.

"Sir," I said, clearing my throat. "Yes . . . I know the rules . . . but this is very very important."

The Penguin dropped his pen and looked up at me. He didn't say anything for a moment.

"Okay. Five minutes. Come in and close the door, please."

I stepped into the office and thought I was going to faint from nervousness. Sitting down on the squeaky leather seat, I felt like the room was spinning. And I had no idea what I was going to say.

"So let's have it, Chris," the Penguin demanded, leaning back in his chair.

"Sure," I said, my throat tightening up. "Well, we . . . I mean I . . . well . . . here. Maybe you should read this first."

I got up and placed the note on his desk.

"What is it?" the Penguin said, but didn't wait for my answer. He flipped the sheet around and began to read.

As his eyes scanned the page, I watched his face for a reaction. His forehead wrinkled. Finally he lifted his eyes and glared at me. "Exactly which students are involved in this?"

"Um," I said, "it's . . . well . . . it's really just . . . me."

"I wanted honesty, Chris," he demanded, placing his index finger on the resolution. "This is signed by the Revolutionists. And I really don't like the language in here."

"Yes, well," I said, taking a deep breath. "The thing is, it started with a bunch of us, and we were called the

Revolutionists and we were all kind of following these histories. I was following the French Revolution—not the Jacobins, but the Marquis de Lafayette actually—but then one of our members became kind of like a tyrant, which was exactly what we were trying to stop in the first place, so I had to stop him because I realized that revolution is serious and can be dangerous, and history always repeats itself but maybe it shouldn't, because it's not all fun and games, and I guess I'm here now because, it was me and only me who thought that the assembly could be, um, a bit more student-focused."

The Penguin was staring at me. Finally he leaned forward in his chair, placed his elbows on the desk, and put his hands together.

"It sounds like you've learned a lot recently," he said.

"Um, yes," I agreed, "I have."

"I'm inclined to agree with you that student involvement is a desirable thing." He leaned back, crossed his legs, and sighed. "The school assembly is thirty minutes, and there's no room in the daily academic schedule to add time. I'm sorry." He paused. "The assembly is composed of the welcome and school song, which totals seven minutes; the principal's address, eight minutes; teacher announcements, ten; and the student council minutes run for five."

He paused again and then shrugged.

"Well," he continued, "we can't do anything about the welcome and school song, but at the next staff meeting

I will propose we shave two minutes off the other three sections, including my address." He lifted a finger. "Once every month, you will have six minutes—and only six minutes—to run a program. Any suggestions for what we might call this new segment?"

"Um, the Student Six?" I offered.

"Perfect," he said, smiling. "The Student Six. I like that, Chris. *You* will be in charge of the Student Six, which will be a student-run program. It can be anything student-focused, but it has to be appropriate." He paused and leaned even farther forward. "It will be a big responsibility, Chris. Are you sure you can handle it?"

"Yes, sir," I said, standing up. "Definitely."

"But just hold on now," he said, putting his hands up. "I have some conditions."

"Okay," I said, still standing.

"You must create a small team of students to help out, and you need to convince a staff member to be an adviser."

"Mr. Evans," I said.

"Yes, that might work well," he said, nodding. "By next Monday, I'll expect you to tell me which students you've gathered to help you lead the Student Six. Also, you'll need to prepare the programs for the first assemblies, so I'll know exactly what you have in mind. After that, you must report to me one week in advance of each assembly with an outline of your production." He paused and wrinkled his forehead. "And, Chris, I will not hear any more reports from Mrs. Topper regarding your lack of con-centration in class. You understand?"

"Yes, sir."

"And last," he said, putting his hand to his chin and choosing his words carefully, "I will leave it to your discre-tion to choose your team, but I will have to insist that you include one classmate."

"Yes, sir," I said. "Of course. Who?"

"Clouds McFadden."

"Clouds?" I blurted out.

"Yes," he said firmly. "He needs something positive to focus on and he will add a . . . unique perspective to your team."

I winced and then nodded. "Yes, sir. He definitely will."

When I got home, Mom was sitting at the kitchen table.

"Christopher, sit down," she said. "Susan just called."

"Oh. Did she say to call back?"

"No Chris," she said, solemnly. "Susan told me what happened today, and then *everything* else. All of it. Right from your first Revolutionist meeting at the baseball dia-mond."

My stomach dropped. I grabbed the back of the chair, sat down, and didn't say a word.

"And to be honest, this isn't the first time Susan and I have spoken on the phone," Mom admitted. "Susan called about a week ago with some odd questions about Magna history."

I recalled the night Mom sent me to my room after she'd picked up the phone.

Mom shook her head. "I should have known better when Susan asked about the original members and the Magna Charter. Now, I understand why Susan had to tell you, the Revolutionists, about our secrets—she was in a jam—but she really should have come to some former Magna members first. I've made a few quick calls and we are holding an emergency meeting next week sometime. Those HAZE girls really got it wrong."

"Yeah, I know, but Susan just didn't want other Magnas to know how bad it had gotten."

Mom nodded. "Now," she said sternly, "as for your erratic revolutionary behavior these days, I think you, your father, and I should have a serious talk."

"Okay," I said, "but for the record, I didn't really want to be a revolutionist, I just wanted to . . . change things in my life. And Clouds seemed so . . . powerful."

"Well, he was that, wasn't he?" she said, rolling her eyes. "I hope you've learned that too much power is not a good thing."

"Definitely. I get that now, for sure."

"You got caught up in some not-so-positive stuff, Crick," she scolded. "That wasn't nice what you did to Mrs. Topper, no matter how mean she is."

"That's what I said too, but Clouds just ignored me," I explained. "Besides, I didn't even really have a role in Code: Get Nixon."

"Yes, Susan told me," Mom said, nodding. "I also heard that in Code: People Power, Lafayette wanted to start an *Assembly* Revolution."

"Not Lafayette," I said firmly. "Me. And I'm making it happen. I had a meeting with the Pen—with Mr. Dorfman about it today."

"You did?"

"Yes," I said, trying to hold back a proud smile. "Meet the leader of the Student Six. We get six minutes of student-focused stuff every month."

"Wow!" Mom said, leaning over and giving me a big hug, which I didn't fight. "That's amazing, Crick. But that's going to be a lot of work and responsibility."

"I know, Mom," I said, standing up and grabbing my bag. "So I need to start brainstorming, but before I do, I have to recruit my first group member. Am I ungrounded from the phone yet?"

"Yes," she said, "but we are still going to have that conversation. And choose your members carefully this time, Crick. You now know how important the right teammate can be."

"Yes," I said, smiling, "I do."

28

I stared at the phone in my attic for a good ten minutes before I picked it up. When I finally did lift the receiver and dial, my heart began to pound. The phone rang and rang, and I was about to hang up when a familiar voice answered the phone.

"Mike McFadden here."

"Um, hi," I said. "It's Chris Stren again. Um, is Clouds there?"

"Chris," he said, then paused. "What a coincidence. We were just talking about giving you call."

"You were?"

"One sec, Chris."

There was a minute of murmuring and then fumbling of the phone. Another pause was followed by a familiar clearing of the throat. "Um, hello?"

The voice was Clouds's but somehow it seemed different.

"Hi Clouds," I said. "It's Chris."

"Oh, hi there, buddy," he said, sounding nervous. "I'm glad you called . . . I had some thoughts I wanted to share with you, but I was hoping to have a bit more time to choose the right words. I feel that, well, I feel I might have sort of overstepped, well not actually overstepped, let's just say—"

"Clouds," I interrupted.

"Yes."

"I have a proposal for you, and you can either take it or leave it."

There was a pause.

"Okay," he said.

"I met with the Penguin after school today and showed him the assembly resolution. Boris and Susan got me a bunch of teachers' signatures, and the Penguin agreed to give us six minutes of Assembly every month until the end of the year."

There was another pause.

"Clouds?"

"Sorry, yeah, all I can say is . . . wow."

"Thanks, I couldn't have done it without help from the others," I said, staying firm, "but I'm now in charge of putting a new team together and . . . I thought of you."

"You did?" he said. There was a long silence on the line. "After all that crazy Lenin stuff I did . . . and all the mean things I said?"

"Yes," I said, considering. "I thought . . . I thought I'd try to bring together some of the most creative, daring, open-minded people at Laverton Middle School."

Clouds laughed, sounding relieved. "Nice one."

"There's only one thing I need you to promise me," I demanded, "before I invite you on the team."

"Anything. You name it, buddy."

"Okay," I said, "if this whole leadership thing goes to my head, and I decide to go all Vlads and tyrannical on you guys, you will be the first to step in and remind me how seriously bad and dangerous that can get."

There was another long pause, and then Clouds said softly, "Yeah . . . I can definitely do that."

"Good," I said.

"One thing though," he said. "When you said 'you guys,' did you mean the rest of the Revolutionists will be joining us?"

I laughed. "Yeah, I hope so. But we have a new name: it's the Student Six. Six minutes of Assembly and six members. I thought Doug in Mr. McNally's class would be a good sixth member to round out our team. Jocks are people too, right?"

Clouds giggled. "No arguments here. And anyway, you're the boss, Chris."

"Actually," I said, smiling, "I prefer to think of this as a collaboration."

Not five minutes after I hung up with Clouds, the phone rang.

"Hello?" I answered.

"Chris," Susan said, excited. "There's an emergency. Can you meet at Sterling Woods?"

"What's going on?"

"I can't explain now. See you there in twenty minutes?"

"Yeah, I'll try my best."

"See you there."

I flew down my ladder, and found Mom in the kitchen.

"Mom, can I go meet Susan for a while?"

She turned from the counter and smiled. "Of course, hon. A good choice for your first teammate! Dinner will be in an hour and a half."

"Thanks, Mom," I said, grabbing my coat, putting on my boots, and flying out the door.

When I turned at the Happy Holiday sign, I was out of breath. I'd run the whole way wondering what Susan wanted to talk about. I slowed to a walk and trudged between birches, following our old footprints to the maple. Under the tree, the snowy ground was all trampled down in a small circle, but Susan wasn't there yet. I leaned against the tree and closed my eyes, remembering our meetings here, and how much had changed since we first met at the baseball diamond. I thought about Clouds on his first day, his feet on Mrs. Topper's desk, his confrontation with the Penguin about the rules, and his risky courting of the Magnas. It all made sense now, like everything was meant to happen the way it did.

"Has Boris been giving you mediation tips or something?"

My heart leaped and I opened my eyes. Susan was standing just feet in front of me.

"You scared me," I said, grabbing my heart. "I was just thinking about how all this crazy stuff got started."

"I can't blame you," Susan said, smiling. "I've been doing a lot of that lately." She paused. "I think I'm able to, like, see Queen Elizabeth and the whole Magna thing a bit more clearly."

"What do you mean? Is that what this meeting is about?"

"Um, sort of," she said, looking down. "Let's go over the history first: Queen Elizabeth wasn't a revolutionist, Chris. She was a queen in power, for goodness sake. Second of all, even though she was a great leader, she was actually ruthless. At the end of the day, Queen Elizabeth was all about power, and that's not what I wanted for myself or for the Magnas. We needed to return to secrecy, equality, and respect."

"And I guess that's where my mom came in."

"Yeah," Susan said, blushing and looking down. "Sorry I had to do that, and that I called her earlier. But I guess you'll have to get used to it—us Magnas are supposed to be secret."

"I can do that," I said, smiling.

"I've also realized that the teachers aren't really that bad when it comes down to it, even if they're not perfect all the time. It's just like when Clouds went crazy with all of his power. Teachers aren't tyrants, it's just that sometimes they're a bit forgetful of their power."

"Yeah," I said, laughing, "and the Penguin definitely doesn't deserve to have his head chopped off in the guillotine, like King Louis the Sixteenth did. In fact . . . the

Penguin is a lot more open-minded then I thought. He actually bent the rules for me today."

"The Penguin bent the rules?"

"Yeah," I said. "He let me have a meeting with him and he agreed to give the students six minutes of assembly time every month!"

"Oh my gosh," Susan said, clapping her hands. "That's so amazing! So you got the resolution in your locker!"

"Yeah, you sneak," I joked. "You didn't tell me you were getting all those signatures."

"Sorry, I totally forgot about it. Last week I went ballistic and got three of them after school, and then stuffed it into my bag. It wasn't until yesterday that I found it. I was going to tell you at break on Tuesday, but there was so much going on.

"Anyway," she said, stepping toward me and putting a hand on my arm, "for the record, I wanted you to know. I'm really done with replaying Queen Elizabeth's history—I've been done with it since we had hot chocolates at Trudy's."

"But what about the Ten Mile Skate and Carina's brother?"

"I called him on Sunday morning and told him I didn't want to go with him."

"But Carina—wasn't she mad?"

"No," Susan said, laughing. "Not at all. Her brother drives her crazy, and she couldn't care less who he dates."

"Wow! That was seriously risky."

"Well, so's this," she said, taking a small step closer. "I am officially tossing away my crown . . . and going after my Robert Dudley."

"Um," I said, blushing, "but I, um, still don't know who that other guy Babington is."

"Look him up in the history books someday," she said, smiling. "So? What do you say to the Queen? I mean to *me*. Will you be my . . . um . . . boyfriend?"

I didn't know what to do. Or say.

Then it came to me.

I grabbed Susan's hand and said, "Your wish is my command!"

Susan laughed. "Harriet was right about one thing," she said.

"What?" I said, standing up close to her.

"You *are* a romantic," she said.

"And not nice?"

"Yes, nice and strong," she said and then kissed me on the cheek.

Epilogue

fter dinner that night, I went straight to the book-
shelf for a handful of encyclopedia volumes. I had
some personal research to do. I absolutely had to know
who Susan's Babington was and who Clouds's Mensheviks
were. I went up to my attic and curled up on my couch.
I opened up the "B" volume, found the right spot, and
began poring over the pages.

Mystery, sabotage, and treason—it was an amazing story. History shouldn't be repeated, but it definitely
should be read.